Promise My Love

A Braden Novella

Love in Bloom Series

Melissa Foster

Cover Design: Natasha Brown & Elizabeth Mackey
Cover Image: Jimmy Thomas

WORLD LITERARY PRESS
PRINTED IN THE UNITED STATES OF AMERICA

A Note to Readers

Loyal, wealthy, and wickedly naughty, that's the definition of our Bradens, and Rex Braden never disappoints. His love for Jade Johnson knows no boundaries, as you'll see in PROMISE MY LOVE, the follow-up novella to DESTINED FOR LOVE (The Bradens).

If this is your first Braden book, then you have a whole series of loyal, sexy, and wickedly naughty Bradens to catch up with. You might enjoy starting with SISTERS IN LOVE, the first of the Love in Bloom series. The characters from each series make appearances in future books. Please visit my website for details on the full Love in Bloom series including a family tree, reading order, and publication schedule.
www.MelissaFoster.com/RG

I'm super excited to bring you the Bradens at Peaceful Harbor, second cousins to the Bradens at Weston. **Sign up for my newsletter** so you never miss a release.
www.MelissaFoster.com/Newsletter

Be sure to check out my online bookstore for pre-orders, early releases, bundles, and exclusive discounts on ebooks, print, and audiobooks. Ebooks can be sent to the e-reader of your choice and audiobooks can be listened to on the free and easy-to-use BookFunnel app. Shop my store: shop.melissafoster.com

Thanks for reading!
Melissa

Chapter One

JADE JOHNSON TRIED to concentrate on what Caitlyn Ray, the florist she'd hired for her wedding, was saying, but she couldn't think past the idea that in three days the handsome cowboy sitting across from her was going to be her husband. Just a few years ago she didn't think anything would ever end the feud between their two families. Who would have guessed that Rex Braden's love for Jade would finally bring their stubborn fathers' walls down so they could be together? Rex had given the feuding men an ultimatum—love them as a couple or lose them forever. Jade hadn't seen the threat coming, and she'd been terrified of how their fathers would react. She'd loved Rex from afar for almost fifteen years—and because of his courage to stand up to their fathers, she'd been able to love him up close for the last four. She couldn't wait to spend the rest of her life falling even deeper in love with the most courageous, loving man on the planet.

"The roses, lilies, and orchids will be gorgeous. We have everything under control. Your wedding will be perfect." Caitlyn flashed a smile that Jade was sure to put most brides' minds at ease, but Jade was still too excited about marrying Rex to be anywhere near *at ease*.

Rex squeezed Jade's hand. "See, babe? Caitlyn's got it covered. Now you can relax." His hands were big and square and as powerful as the rest of his mountainous body.

Rex was the most beautiful man Jade had ever known, inside and out, a gentleman to his very core. He was also the most seductive, talented lover Jade had ever had. Even after four years, the passion between them hadn't dimmed. She flushed just thinking about how intense their lovemaking had been that morning, first in the bedroom, then in the shower, and when Jade still hadn't had enough of him, *she'd* seduced *him* while he attempted to clothe all his magnificent muscles. She'd never get enough of him. They'd been living together for four years, and she couldn't wait to get married and start their family. She'd worried lately that she might have trouble getting pregnant. There was no reason for concern. Her doctor had assured her of that when she'd gone off the pill. But still, she worried. Her mother had wanted a big family, as many as six, like her best friend, Adriana Braden—Rex's mother—had had, but she'd been blessed with only two children, Jade and her brother, Steven. Her mother was in good health otherwise, while Adriana had died of cancer when Rex was just a boy, leaving him and his five siblings to be raised by their father, Hal.

Jade pushed aside the worry and told herself to think positively. She and Rex wanted a big family. But when it came to family, Rex had old-fashioned values, and he'd been clear about his feelings of weddings coming before babies. In three days they'd have that first box checked off. Then time would tell if babies were in their future.

"...so as I was saying, I'm confident that we won't have any issue."

Jade realized Caitlyn was speaking to her. "Great. Thank

you."

Caitlyn leaned closer to Rex and pointed to his necklace. "That is the most unique necklace I've ever seen."

Rex pushed his Stetson farther back on his thick black hair, and his lips curved into a proud smile as he touched the charm.

"This necklace has a very special meaning to us. It's the Dance of Two Lovers." He draped an arm around Jade's shoulder and kissed her temple.

"Legend has it that everything in their lives was meant to keep them apart, and against all odds, they found their way to each other. Just like me and Jade. Supposedly, when the two lovers danced, their souls became one, and from that moment on, they lived within each other no matter if they were together or apart."

He gazed into Jade's eyes, and the worry she held melted away. He had that effect on her. His love was an elixir, a remedy for all things that needed healing.

"The charms come together to form two bodies intertwined," Rex explained. "Jade wears the other half, and we never take them off. They were once my mother's." The myth fit them perfectly. When Rex and Jade had finally come together, they'd had to carry out their relationship in secret so as not to upset their parents. Until one day when Rex couldn't take the secrecy anymore—and to Jade's surprise, the painful confrontation that had taken place between Rex and their parents had finally begun to mend the fence that never should have been broken in the first place.

"May I see yours?" Caitlyn asked.

Jade pushed her long hair from her shoulders and opened the collar of her shirt.

"Um…" Caitlyn's eyes shifted to Rex.

Rex's eyes narrowed with confusion. Jade touched her neck. "Oh God." She felt frantically for the necklace. "Rex? Where is it?" She pulled open her shirt and peered into her bra, then stood and scanned the floor. She couldn't have lost it. Not now, three days before their wedding. The necklace was a treasured link to Rex's deceased mother. His father had given the necklace to his mother, and before they'd even been married, she'd given it to a high school friend with the message that she'd know who it was for. More than twenty-five years later, Jade and Rex had walked into an eclectic shop in the Village in Allure, Colorado, and the owner had instinctively known the necklace was meant for them. She'd tucked it away all those years ago when Adriana had given it to her. Jade would never forget the way Rex had lost his breath, broken out in a cold sweat, and collapsed into a chair when he'd seen the necklace. That was the moment he'd confessed that he was falling in love with Jade, and their love had grown stronger ever since. The necklace symbolized the strength of their love, and now it was gone.

Jade had a sinking feeling in the pit of her stomach.

Rex was on his feet, searching the floor beneath the table where they'd been sitting and then all the way to the front door. "We'll find it, babe."

"Maybe it came off in the shower? Mine do that sometimes and I don't notice until it's gone down the drai—" Caitlyn bit her lower lip. "Oh, yikes. That's not helpful. I'm sure that's not what happened."

Jade felt her eyes well with tears. "Rex?"

His arms encircled her, and he drew her against his muscular chest. "It's okay, babe. We'll find it. We'll go home and retrace your steps." At six foot three, Rex towered over Jade. She'd always felt safe in his arms, his heart beating against her cheek, sure and strong. If she'd lost their cherished necklace, she wondered how *he* could ever trust her again.

Her cell phone rang, and she dug it out of her purse. "It's my mom. Maybe the necklace fell off during dinner last night and she found it." She answered the call filled with hope.

"Hi, Mom."

"Honey…" Her mother's voice was thin, strangled.

"Mom? What's wrong?" Jade felt Rex's hand grip her shoulder.

"It's…your father."

Her mother paused, and Jade heard her crying. Tears sprang from Jade's eyes as she imagined the worst. Her father was a big man at three hundred pounds, and she'd feared for his health for a long time.

"Mom? What happened?" She looked up at Rex, and his arms came around her again. Jade listened as her mother told her that her father was in the hospital. He'd had a heart attack. They were still waiting for a prognosis. Jade's legs weakened, her heart shattered, and the phone crashed to the floor as her world spiraled out of control.

Chapter Two

HOURS AFTER ARRIVING at the hospital, Rex stood beside Earl Johnson's hospital bed with one arm around Jade, the other around Jane Johnson, Jade's mother. There was a time when Earl had despised Rex simply because he was Hal Braden's son. Hal was a highly respected horse breeder in Weston, Colorado, and was one of the wealthiest men around. He and Earl had been close when they were growing up, but when Earl fell on hard times, he'd been too proud to ask Hal for financial help, and he'd gone behind Hal's back and trusted the dirtiest horse trader in the business—a man who had done everything he could to keep Hal and Adriana apart. Buying horses from that man had been the fuel behind the forty-year feud between the Bradens and the Johnsons. Rex remembered the night he'd stood up to the two men, supported by his brothers standing behind him as a united force.

It had been a long, hard road to reconciliation, but it was worth every heated moment. Now, as Rex held Jade, the woman he loved most in the world, and Jane, the woman who had been his mother's best friend until the day she'd died—including several years when they'd kept their friendship hidden from their feuding husbands—he couldn't imagine a life without any of them. Earl was a bullheaded man, but his love for his family was never ending. He'd raised Jade and her brother with morals and purpose, and Rex was reaping the benefits. Jade was the most loving woman he'd ever known. She was smart as a whip and stubborn as a mule, which was good, because Rex was a broody man and he often needed Jade's gumption to set him straight. He smiled, thinking about how many times her smile had melted his determination. And her touch—holy hell, her seductive touch—he was always putty in her hands.

Jade held her father's hand in both of hers. He'd come out of surgery a few hours ago, after having a stent put in. The surgery had disrupted his heartbeat, and they'd had to give him an external pacemaker as well. He had a line going into his groin from the pacemaker, which was now strapped to his thigh. It was strange how a hospital gown could diminish the severity of a man's presence.

"Daddy, how are you feeling? Are you in any pain?"

"I'm okay, darlin'. Just tired. Don't you worry about me. You just keep getting ready for your wedding. I'll be fine."

"Earl, we're postponing the wedding," Rex said.

Earl shifted his blue-gray eyes to Rex. His jowls swallowed any hint of the neck he'd once had. "You are not to do any such thing. My baby girl is walking down that aisle on Sunday."

"But, Dad, I want you to give me away." Jade looked up at Rex, her blue eyes pooled with worry.

He'd waited four long years to marry Jade. He'd wanted her to have the perfect life. With Jade he was a whole different man than he was around anyone else. She'd softened all his rough edges and had unveiled a romantic side of himself he'd never known existed. He'd wanted her to have the perfect wedding and had even tried to plan it, but Jade wanted to plan her own wedding. At least they'd agreed on the importance of having the wedding at his father's ranch, which Rex had run for the past twenty years. He had visions of Jade riding up on Flame, her stallion, and Hope, his mother's aging horse, standing calmly by. They would be surrounded by both of their families, on the same grounds where his parents had raised him.

Family knows no boundaries. It was the Braden family creed, and Rex had lived loyally by it forever. He knew how important it was for Jade to have her father walk her down the aisle, but the worried look in Earl's eyes told Rex that Earl might be worried about his poor health catching up to him in an even worse way than it already had.

"Looks like I'm late to the party." Jade's brother walked into the room with a serious look in his eyes.

Jade jumped to her feet and flew into Steve's arms. "You're here."

"You knew I would be." Steve was tall and broad, with shaggy dark hair that looked out of place with his park ranger uniform. He worked in the mountains of Preston, Colorado, two towns away.

Steve hugged his mother. "You okay, Mom?"

Jane's frail shoulders rounded forward as if she'd lost all her strength. Even her brown hair had gone limp. She reached down and set a hand on her husband's arm. "As well as can be expected."

"He's a strong man, Mom. He'll be okay." Steve embraced Rex next. "Rex, still as big as a bear, I see."

Rex laughed. "Look who's talking. You're looking fit…for a *mountain* man."

Steve was a big man, but at six foot three, two hundred fifty pounds, Rex had him beat by at least fifty pounds of solid muscle.

"I hear I'm going to be working with your cousin Shannon on an environmental project," Steve said.

"Second cousin, and I'll be watching you, so best keep yourself in line," Rex warned. Shannon was in her early twenties and pretty as the day was long. She lived in Peaceful Harbor, Maryland, and was staying with Hal for the summer to complete a research assignment.

"Shit." Steve scoffed. "I haven't even met her yet. No need to get your panties in a bunch." He leaned over his father and kissed his balding head. "How you feeling, Pop?"

"I've seen better days." Earl patted his son's hand. "Looks like the baby doc followed you in. Any news, Benji?"

Dr. Ben Carpenter shook his head as he came to Earl's side. Ben had taken over his father's medical practice after his father had retired. Mason Carpenter had been the town cardiologist for longer than Rex had been alive. No matter how successful Ben was, or how old he became, the old-timers still thought of him as little Ben, or as Earl had said, *Benji.*

"How about we stick to calling me either *Ben* or *Dr. Carpenter*," Ben suggested with an arched brow and a slight smile.

"Dr. Carpenter was your father, but I suppose I can manage *Ben*," Earl said.

Rex held a hand out and Ben shook it. "Good to see you, Ben."

"You too, Rex. How's Hal?"

"Doing great, thanks. Would you like privacy for this conversation? I can wait out in the hall." Rex pointed a thumb over his shoulder toward the hall.

Jade reached for him. "No. Please stay."

"Earl?" Rex asked out of respect for his future father-in-law.

Earl nodded. "My girl wants you here. I think you've got your answer."

"Okay, well, Earl, hopefully this stent will do well for you," Ben said. "You had one artery that was ninety percent blocked, which was actually lucky. It could have been worse. The stent should keep that open. But as I explained to your wife, your heartbeat was a little irregular, so we put you on an external pacemaker. Hopefully, we'll be able to remove that in twenty-four hours. We'll get you up and around once the pacemaker is removed." Ben crossed his arms and lowered his chin, setting serious eyes on Earl. "We're going to keep you here for a couple days of monitoring to make sure you don't run into any other issues, but you should be able to go home Saturday afternoon. And I plan on harping on you each and every day about diet and exercise until you listen."

Earl grumbled something indiscernible. "Saturday? See that, baby girl? I'll be able to walk you down the aisle after all."

"Excuse me, Earl," Rex said. "What if there are complications and you don't make it out of the hospital? I still think we should postpone the wedding, just to be safe." The idea of unforeseen circumstances arising with Earl's health and Jade being disappointed on Sunday was crushing.

Earl pointed a chubby finger at him. "Rex, you are *not* postponing this wedding." He shifted his eyes to Jade. "Darlin', if you delay your wedding, it will be that man's head rolling when I'm strong enough to take him down, and don't you doubt that one day I will most definitely be strong enough to do it."

Ben placed a hand on Earl's shoulder. "Settle down, Earl. You're supposed to be healing, not mandating how your daughter and Rex live their lives. I'm sure they can work out their own wedding."

"Nothing to work out," Earl grumbled, and shot a narrow-eyed look at Rex.

"Well, we do have the whole wedding planned," Jade said. "If Ben thinks Dad will be out in time, then I can't see why we should postpone it."

Rex had been brought up to respect his elders, but this didn't feel right to him. He wouldn't take a chance of getting married if his father were in the hospital, but he knew Jade had been planning the wedding for months, and Jade's needs had trumped his own since their very first kiss.

"I don't like this, Jade," Rex said. "Family has to come first, and you're under enough stress already. But if this is what you want…"

"Thank you." Jade rose to her feet and kissed his cheek. "I trust Ben's judgment." She leaned in close to Rex and whispered, "I want to get some information about his dietary restrictions."

"Ben, can I talk to you a minute outside?" Jade grabbed Ben's arm and dragged him out the door.

"Earl, I'm with Rex on this," Jane said. "Jade will be devastated if you can't walk her down that aisle, and who knows what will happen between now and then."

"Now, sweet pea, we both know that there are no guarantees in this world." Earl reached for his wife's hand. "Please do not let our daughter put her life on hold for me. If I'm able, I'll be at that wedding." He slid a steely gaze to Rex, leaving no room for negotiation.

Rex knew that there was no arguing with Earl. He had a feeling that pushing the issue would put him on the cusp of another family feud.

Chapter Three

IT WAS DARK by the time Rex headed back to his father's ranch to check on the animals. He walked into the barn and inhaled the familiar scent of leather and hay. It was a comforting smell, one that Rex had been around his whole life. He found his eldest brother, Treat, in the barn with Hope. Rex had called Treat and asked him to take over the evening chores around the ranch in case he didn't get back in time. Treat and Rex each owned property adjacent to their father's ranch. While Rex worked on the ranch full-time, Treat helped out as needed and still ran his resort business from his home office.

"How's Earl?" Treat stood beside Hope with a concerned look in his dark eyes. He was six foot six, like their father, with thick black hair that he kept cropped short. Treat owned resorts all over the world, and before meeting his wife, Max, he'd traveled more than eighty percent of the year. When he fell in love with Max, he put down roots here in Weston, so she could continue working for the Colorado Indie Film Festival, a job she loved. That was, until they had their two children, Adriana, now five, and their baby, Dylan. Now, while they raised their children, Max worked remotely from home and Treat traveled only six to eight times each year.

"As ornery as ever. They put in a stent, and they're going to monitor him for a few days. They had to hook up an external pacemaker, so I guess we'll see." Rex righted his Stetson and moved in front of Hope. The red mare was getting up in age. Patches of white fur were becoming more evident with each passing year. She'd been moving slower lately, and Rex had made the painful decision to stop riding her two weeks ago. It was the first step in letting go, and not a decision he'd come to lightly.

Hope pressed her nose into Rex's solar plexus and he planted a kiss on her broad forehead. Rex loved her up every morning before daybreak, and she was the last horse he said good night to at the end of each day. Hope was special to all of them. She had been a gift from Hal to their mother the year their mother had fallen ill. Hope had remained strong and agile long after their mother's life had been stolen by cancer, a villain that none of them had been strong enough to slay.

Rex stroked Hope's neck and swore her big black eyes looked sad, too. "Jade refuses to delay the wedding."

"How do you feel about it?" Treat asked.

Rex shrugged. "I've waited four years to marry Jade." He stood back from Hope and leaned against the stall. "*Four years*, Treat. In those four years I've watched you have a beautiful daughter and son. I've watched Hugh adopt Layla and bring Christian into the world. Now Savannah's pregnant, and I'm still waiting to start my family with Jade." Rex didn't hold Treat or his younger siblings' good fortune against them, but hell if he wasn't jealous. "I want that, Treat. I want kids. I want Jade as my wife, not just my fiancée. You know that."

"I do know all those things, Rex."

"But now...It's just not right. Earl's family, and Jade's one dream is to have her father walk her down the aisle. You know that anything can go wrong. I just feel like shit about waiting so long to get married in the first place, but Jade wanted to plan the wedding, and she was so busy with her veterinary practice, and now…" Rex took off his hat and ran his hand through his long black hair.

"Am I a prick for wanting to postpone the wedding? I feel like a prick. Something in Earl's eyes told me that he was worried about waiting, like he wasn't sure he'd make it much longer—though Ben thinks he will get out of the hospital on Saturday. We're three days from our wedding, and both Jade and Earl want this wedding to take place, but I look at Earl and he's hooked up to a pacemaker and all these monitors and machines."

"Talk to Jade. Maybe she'll come to see it your way." Treat petted Hope again.

Rex arched a brow. "You do remember my fiancée, right? Hot little number with a big heart and a bigger stubborn streak."

"I don't envy you. I wouldn't want to go up against Earl, much less Jade. Remember, she's waited years to marry you, too. I'm sure she's overwhelmed and clutching to Ben's prognosis for her sanity. Give it a day."

"She is overwhelmed. Which is another reason I think we should postpone the wedding. What would you do?"

"That depends on which is the lesser of two evils: pissing off Jade and her father or possibly watching your fiancée's dream of having her father walk her down the aisle fall apart on her wedding day." Treat paused, looking intently at Hope as that truth settled in. "You think Hope looks okay?"

"She looks a little off to me, but it may be my slant on things at the moment. Where's Dad?" Their father swore by the very ground he walked on that their mother watched over Hope from beyond the grave. If anyone could tell if Hope was okay or not, it would be Hal.

"He went to bed early after visiting Earl." Treat smiled. "Funny how far they've come. I never thought I'd see the day when Dad visited Earl anywhere."

As they walked up the hill toward Rex's truck, Rex remembered the necklace Jade had lost. They had breakfast most mornings with Treat's family and Hal at Hal's house, and he wondered if it had fallen off there.

"You haven't seen Jade's necklace, have you?" Everyone in the family knew about the special connection Rex and Jade had to the necklace. It was the only necklace either of them ever wore.

Treat slowed his pace. "No, but I'll keep an eye out. She lost it?"

"Apparently." Rex's chest constricted at the thought that the necklace might be lost forever.

"I'm sorry, Rex. I'll ask Max to look around, too."

"Thanks. I'm going to scour our place, then retrace her steps since the last time she remembers having it on." Rex headed for his truck, then turned back. "Hey, Treat, you know I'm happy for you and Max, and Hugh and Bree, and Savannah and Jack, right? I was just venting my frustrations, but—"

"Rex, I get it. And don't worry. You guys will figure this out."

He was sure they would, but standing on the opposite side of Earl and Jade was not someplace Rex wanted to spend a single second, much less the next few days.

JADE CALLED RILEY Banks, her best friend—and fiancée to Rex's brother Josh—while she searched the house for her necklace. It was after eleven, and Rex was checking on the animals at his father's ranch. She knew Riley wouldn't care if she called at three o'clock in the morning, much less one o'clock in the morning, as it was now in New York. As her maid of honor, she practically expected late-night freak-outs.

"Hey, future bride. Are you overwhelmingly nervous about Sunday?" Riley and Josh were world-renowned fashion designers and lived in New York City. They had a fashion show this weekend, but they were flying back to Colorado late Saturday afternoon for Sunday's wedding.

"Ri, I'm not sure there's going to be a wedding."

"What? Jade, what's going on? Do you want me to come home right now? I'll blow off the show if you're desperate for me to smack you upside your head."

She heard the smile in Riley's voice. "Dad's in the hospital. He had a heart attack."

"Oh, no. I'm so sorry." And just like that, a warm hug came through the phone. "I'll come home."

"No. Stay for your show. It's fine. He's supposed to get out of the hospital Saturday. He doesn't want us to delay the wedding, but of course Rex thinks we should. He can't fathom the idea of having the wedding with Dad in the hospital. I just don't know what to do." Tears welled in her eyes. She felt like she'd done nothing but cry lately.

"How bad is he? What did Ben say?" One of the most comforting things about living in a small town was also one of the most annoying—everyone knew everyone else. In this case, it was a good thing, because Riley knew and trusted Ben. He'd been a few years ahead of them in school.

"They put in a stent and an external pacemaker to regulate his heartbeat. Ben thinks Dad will get out on Saturday and he should recover fine. There was only blockage in one artery, which is surprising given how he eats. Of course he needs lifestyle changes. He's needed them forever." Jade sighed. "You know Dad. He's never going to stop eating Mom's corn bread loaded with butter, or spare ribs, or pie…"

"Well, it's good news that he'll recover. Your mom must be a mess. Are you sure you don't want me to come home and help you? The show means nothing to me compared to your family."

"No. We're okay. Mom spent half the day like a zombie, but you know her. She'll be stronger once the initial shock wears off. I am worried about how we're going to convince Dad to eat healthier and exercise."

"Maybe it's time for your mom to modify her cooking habits without telling him. Why don't you talk to Max and see if she can give her some tips. She knows all about swapping butter for applesauce and other heart-friendly tips. When we were down at Christmas, she was telling me all about the substitutions she makes for Hal because Treat worries about his heart."

"That man is stronger than a bull." Jade made a mental note to ask Max tomorrow.

"Yeah, but he's almost seventy, and according to Max, Ben told Treat that big men—heavy or tall—tend to have more trouble as they age. Jade, I'm happy to come home. I don't want you to go through this alone."

"I'm fine. Rexy is here, and even if he's upset about not canceling the wedding, he's still my rock." She thought about the necklace, and more tears sprang to her eyes. "Ri?"

"Yeah?"

"There's something else." Jade nibbled on her lower lip.

"More than your dad's heart attack?"

Jade heard Riley cover the mouthpiece and say, "Josh, I might have to go home tomorrow."

"Stop. You are *not* missing your show," Jade said. Riley and Josh had been preparing for the fashion show for the past eight months.

"I'll be the judge of that. What else?"

"His mom's necklace." She couldn't bring herself to say it.

"Oh God, Jade. What?"

"I lost it," she whispered.

"No. No way. Did you look everywhere?"

"Yeah." She looked around the messy bedroom. She'd torn through every drawer, her entire closet, the bathroom, and she'd left everything upended. "You should see our bedroom. It looks like we've been robbed. I turned the house upside down."

"Okay. I'm sure we'll find it. If you haven't found it by the time I arrive, I'll retrace your steps, too. For now just breathe." Riley paused, and Jade imagined her brows knitted and her eyes darting around the room as if she might conjure up the necklace from afar. "Did you check your car? The barn? Hal's barn? Your clients' barns?"

"Not yet, but I will tomorrow. It's been a crazy day with Dad landing in the hospital." Jade heard the door open and Rex's heavy footsteps crossing the hardwood floor, and the air immediately felt lighter. She listened to his footfalls on the stairs. "Rexy's home. I want to see him. I'll call you tomorrow."

"Are you sure you don't want me to come home?"

Rex's broad shoulders filled the bedroom doorway as his dark eyes skirted over the upended room. The right side of his mouth quirked up in a sexy smile that made Jade's heart flutter. He closed the distance between them, every step full of stealth and virility that she was sure only Rex Braden could pull off.

His eyes narrowed, darkened, as they shifted to the phone.

"Ri?" Rex whispered when he reached the edge of the bed.

Jade nodded. "Ri, I've…" Her mouth went dry when he tugged his shirt over his head and tossed it aside, revealing the peaks and valleys of his ripped abs and muscular chest. "Ri?" Her body tingled with anticipation as she watched him tug off his boots and unhook his belt.

"Oh my God, he's taking his clothes off, isn't he?" Riley laughed. "I swear our Braden boys know what we like. Call me if you need me, and give my love to your mom and dad." Riley ended the call, and Jade set the phone on the bedside table.

Rex stepped from his jeans and crawled across the mattress like a panther on the prowl, his bulbous muscles emphasizing the depth of his power. His eyes simmered with passion, stealing the last of her rational thought. He crawled over her, bringing her down beneath him. His hard length pressed firmly against her center as he laced his hands with hers.

"I missed you, baby," he rasped against her neck, sending shivers of heat through her body.

"I couldn't find the necklace." She didn't know why she felt the need to confess that when what she really wanted was to disappear into him.

He touched his forehead to hers and smiled down at her. "It's okay. We'll find it." He kissed her tenderly. "I'm sorry about your dad, babe. Are you okay?"

"I am now."

"I'm going to make sure you're more than okay." He kissed a path between her breasts, gently stripping off each piece of her clothing, leaving her bare and wanting beneath him. He proceeded to do as he promised, loving her with his mouth, his hands, and every inch of his magnificent body until all she felt was pure, unadulterated bliss.

Chapter Four

EARLY THE NEXT morning they awoke to the shrill ring of a cell phone. Jade nearly jumped out of her skin as she clamored to get her phone.

"Oh God. Dad," she said as she climbed across Rex and grabbed her phone. She quickly looked over at Rex's nightstand when she realized it wasn't her phone ringing.

"It's mine, babe." Rex pulled her into his arms as he reached for his phone. "It's Dane, not your dad. Come here." He lay back against the pillow, bringing Jade down with him and holding her against his chest as he answered the call.

"Dane? Is something wrong?" Rex's older brother Dane was an expert on sharks. As the founder of the Brave Foundation, whose mission was to use education and innovative advocacy programs to protect sharks, he and his fiancée, Lacy, traveled often.

"Lacy's been sick all evening. I just wanted to give you a heads-up. It's probably the flu. We'll see how she feels tomorrow before making any decisions, but we may not make the wedding."

"Dane, it's four thirty in the morning here. Where are you? Is Lacy okay?"

"Australia. We're on a tagging assignment. I think she'll be fine. It's just the flu or something. I totally forgot about the time difference. Sorry about that."

"No worries. It's cool. Let us know about Lacy, and give her our best. Earl is in the hospital. He had a heart attack."

"Oh, damn. I'm sorry we're not there with you guys. Is he going to pull through?"

Rex explained Earl's prognosis and that he should get out of the hospital on Saturday.

"Rex, are you going to postpone the wedding?"

Rex looked at Jade lying across his chest in a silky negligee. Her brows were knitted together. He imagined she was thinking about her father. All Rex had ever wanted was to make her happy, and if Sunday came and her father was still in the hospital, he'd never forgive himself for not pushing her to agree to postpone. He kissed the top of Jade's head, wishing he knew which way to go—insist they delay the wedding or let things play out and hope for the best?

"Jade and Earl don't want to postpone it." Saying it aloud felt even more uncomfortable than thinking about it. He needed to get off the phone so he could breathe. "Give my love to Lacy, and let us know how she's feeling tomorrow."

He ended the call and closed his eyes, feeling Jade's finger drawing a path down the left side of his chest.

"Hey, babe, Lacy's sick. They're not sure if they'll make it to the wedding."

"Oh no. I hope she feels better soon." She propped her chin on Rex's chest and gazed up at him.

He hadn't realized that he'd been hoping that might make her change her mind. Rex slid out from beneath her and sat on the edge of the bed, his muscles tense from a fitful night's sleep.

"I really think we should postpone the wedding."

He felt Jade's strong, soft hands on his shoulders as she kneaded his tension away. In addition to being a veterinarian, Jade was a specialist in equine shiatsu and acupuncture. The way she was touching Rex brought back memories of the way she'd touched him when they were first dating. No one had ever touched Rex with as much love and tenderness, as much intense passion, as Jade had that night—and every day since.

He reached up and placed his hand on hers, knowing he'd do anything she wanted, including not canceling the wedding.

Later that morning, after checking on the horses, Rex came back home to pick up Jade for breakfast and found her sitting in her office leafing through photo albums. Jade, like Rex, wasn't big on technology. They both used cell phones and computers, but Jade still preferred to have her photographs printed by a camera shop rather than downloading them from a phone onto her computer. She'd kept albums from the time she was in grade school.

"Feeling sentimental?" Rex leaned down and kissed her cheek. She smelled like Flame, which told him she'd taken a stroll down to their barn while he was at his father's ranch. She loved that horse as much as she loved him, and he loved that about her, too.

"I was just thinking about the wedding. I always dreamed of my father walking me down the aisle."

Rex crouched beside her. "I know. I called Ben this morning and he said your father is doing well. Chances are he'll be fine to walk you down the aisle Sunday, but I still think postponing the wedding just to be safe is a good idea."

Jade sighed and ran her finger over a picture of her holding her father's hand when she was about ten years old.

"He'll walk me down the aisle. I know he will. Besides, we have everything planned, and…" She nibbled on her lower lip as if she were contemplating saying something else, and when she didn't, Rex tried again to persuade her.

"And what if he's not? What if we go through with it and he's stuck in the hospital? I'll never forgive myself for not pushing you to put it off."

Her eyes teared up, and Rex gathered her in his arms, feeling his own chest tighten over her sadness. He knew she was sad over her father more than the idea of postponing their wedding, but her emotions were all tangled up, and Rex was powerless to separate them and cause her more pain by making the decision himself.

"It's Friday. We have one more day until we have to make a final decision. Let's not worry about it until then. You go spend the day with your dad, and I'll take care of whatever loose ends need to be tied up. I have to get Ross out here to see Hope, too, because she's not doing well." Rex's cousin Ross lived in Trusty, Colorado, and he was also a veterinarian.

"Hope?" Fresh tears sprang to Jade's eyes. "I'll look at her."

"No way. You have enough on your plate. Ross is a great vet, and you need to be with your father."

"Maybe this is all a sign because I lost the necklace. What if this is all my fault? Dad, Hope—"

"Jade, none of this is your fault. Your father was a ticking time bomb. You know that. You've worried about his health for years, and Hope has already lived longer than any horse I've ever had."

She gazed up at him with damp eyes. "What if the necklace was the key to holding it all together—holding us together— and everything falls apart? What if my dad doesn't make it?

What if Hope dies? What if we don't find the necklace? That was your most meaningful tie to your mother, Rexy, and I lost it."

Rex cupped her cheeks and kissed her forehead. The one thing he heard loud and clear was what if the necklace was what held them together, and as wrong as that was, it wasn't the most pressing *what if* she'd asked. "Baby, your father is going to make it. Ben hasn't given us any indication that he thinks otherwise, and Ross will fix Hope up. We'll find the necklace. I'm sure we will." He held her tight and hoped to hell the things he said were true.

Jade rarely cried. She was a strong woman with a sassy personality, and she'd been so emotional these last few days— weeks?—that Rex worried even more. As much as he wanted to postpone the wedding, he was more concerned about causing her any more grief.

"My stomach is a little off this morning. I think I'm going to skip breakfast and go directly to the hospital."

"I'll walk you out." He walked her to the car and pulled her in close. "Babe, you have to know that there is nothing holding us together but the love we feel for each other. Please tell me you know that."

"But—"

He pressed his finger to her lips. "No buts. I love you, and you love me. It's a pretty simple equation. Right now your world feels like it's crumbling around you. It's not. We're solid. I promise you that."

Rex watched her car until it disappeared over the ridge, and he finally breathed again. Would he ever get used to seeing her worry? It cut like a knife, slicing anew with every look.

He pushed those thoughts away and called Ross. They made

plans to meet at the barn later in the afternoon and then Rex drove over to Hal's. He saw Treat heading for the barn with Adriana holding his hand and Dylan snuggled against his shoulder.

"Hold up," Rex called out as he climbed from his truck.

Adriana dropped Treat's hand and ran toward Rex. Even at five she resembled her grandmother, with long brown hair, big, almond-shaped eyes, and always a smile on her slightly wide mouth.

"Uncle Rex! We're going to see Hope." She jumped into his arms and wrapped her skinny arms around his thick neck. She smelled like syrup, and her sticky little hands told him that she'd had her mother's famous pancakes for breakfast.

"Did you eat my pancakes this morning?" Rex teased.

Adriana's hair was pinned up in two ponytails that swung as she shook her head. "Mommy saved you some, but Dylan ate Daddy's."

"He did, did he? That little rascal."

Adriana giggled. "He is a rascal. Why weren't you there for breakfast?"

"I was with Aunt Jade."

She laid her head on Rex's shoulder. "Mommy said Jade's daddy is sick. I hope he feels better soon."

"Me too, princess. Are you excited about being one of the flower girls for our wedding?" Adriana and Layla, Hugh's daughter, were going to be flower girls and walk down the aisle together.

They came to the bottom of the hill, and Rex followed Treat into the barn.

Adriana nodded, eyes wide. "My dress is beautiful. Daddy said I'm going to be the prettiest girl there, but Mommy said I am not supposed to be prettier than the bride, so don't tell Aunt Jade."

"Don't you worry about Aunt Jade. She thinks you're beautiful, too. But I have a feeling you and Layla will be equally as beautiful." Rex kissed her cheek.

She giggled. "Your whiskers are prickly."

He set Adriana down. "Don't get into any trouble."

"Uncle Rex, I never get into trouble." She held on to one of Rex's fingers.

Rex walked up to Hope's stall, and Hope didn't nuzzle against his chest. Her head hung low, and her whole body seemed to sag.

"She's having trouble today," Rex said quietly to Treat as he opened Hope's stall. "I was down earlier and I've already called Ross."

Dylan reached for Rex, and he took him from Treat and kissed his chubby little hand. "How's it going, moose?"

Dylan giggled.

"Dad was down even earlier than you were." Treat's face was somber. Rex could tell that he was worried about Hope, and they were both avoiding the elephant in the room—what would happen to Hal if Hope passed away?

"Where is he now?"

"Up at the house with Max and Shannon. Max is going with him to the hospital in a few minutes, and Shannon's going to watch the kids."

"Good. Jade is already there, and I'm sure she can use the company."

"I talked to Dane this morning," Treat said. "Lacy's been sick. I hope they can still make the wedding."

Treat petted Hope's side, and Hope finally pressed her

muzzle to Rex's chest. Rex's shirts were all worn in the center from that very motion. He was trying to ignore the tug in his heart at the thought of losing Hope.

"I know," Rex said. "He called me at the ass crack of dawn."

Dylan reached for Rex's hat and he handed the toddler his Stetson, which Dylan immediately began sucking on.

"Sorry, moose, no leather snacks today." He slid the hat back on his head, and when Dylan whined, Treat reached into his pocket and pulled out a hard rubber horse, which Dylan was very happy to gnaw on.

"In case I don't tell you often enough, you're a great father, Treat."

"We had a great role model." Treat nodded toward the entrance to the barn, where Max and Hal were closing in on them. Treat opened his arms to Max, and she settled right in against him, dwarfed by his broad frame.

"Heading to the hospital?" Treat asked.

Max's long dark hair fell loosely over her shoulders. She wore jeans and boots, dressed up with a silky tank top. Max smiled up at Treat and went up on her toes to kiss him.

"We are. I just came down to get the kids and bring them up to Shannon so you guys could do manly things without being hamstrung by the kids."

Rex pressed a kiss to Dylan's cheek. "Hamstrung? I love these guys."

Max stroked the back of Dylan's dark head, and he reached for his mommy. She took Dylan from Rex, and he instantly missed the weight of him in his arms. The paternal longing that had gripped him over recent months rose to the surface.

"I know you do, Rex. Maybe after your wedding you and Jade can start a family right away."

"That's the plan." Rex knelt beside Adriana and lifted her up in the air. She squealed and giggled. He kissed her cheek, then set her on her feet. "If we're blessed enough to have children half as wonderful as yours, we'll be in good shape."

Max rolled her eyes. "Please, with yours and Jade's genes, you'll have smart, strong, beautiful babies."

"They'll have stubborn babies." Hal slung an arm over Rex's shoulder. "Stubborn, proud, beautiful babies, like we did."

"Thanks, Dad." Sadness swept through Rex as Jade's father's mortality eked into his thoughts. Hal's hair was now more gray than black. His face was mapped with lines from too many years of toiling under the hot sun. He was still a handsome man, and it was easy for Rex to fool himself into thinking that his father might live forever with his fortitude and commanding air of self-confidence. But with Hope and Earl ailing, real life had a way of creeping in and stripping away the linebacker shoulders and barrel chest and revealing the aging man beneath.

"How's Jade holding up, son?" Hal asked.

"About as good as to be expected. She refuses to postpone the wedding, though, and that isn't sitting well with me." He contemplated telling his father about the necklace, but he didn't want to upset him. He held out hope that they'd eventually find it.

"What does Earl want?" Hal asked.

Rex found it interesting that Hal didn't ask what he wanted, but then again, he and his father talked often, and Rex had made no bones about wanting to marry Jade since the day he'd told their families about them.

"He wants us to go through with it."

"Then, that's what you'll do." Hal went to Hope and kissed her on the top of her head. "Right, Hope?"

Hope neighed and nodded her head.

Rex scoffed. "What about *family comes first* and all that? Besides, what if Earl doesn't get out of the hospital and he can't walk her down the aisle?"

Hal turned serious eyes to his son. "Family does come first, son. The thing is, I don't think Jade wants to take a chance at her father not being there any more than you do. I think her heart is too broken right now to think clearly, but Earl…Well, son, Earl's thinking for her, and there are times in every father's life when he has to step in and do the thinking for his children."

Treat walked Adriana and Dylan out of the barn with Max, then returned to his father's side.

"She's an adult, Dad. I think she's well past that stage," Rex said.

"I've got to tell you, Rex," Treat said. "I know what Dad's talking about. I think Adriana will have a hard time keeping my nose out of her business."

"So I'm supposed to just sit back and go along with it? Call the florist and the caterer and the photographer as if I'm excited to get this wedding off the ground? And what about Dane and Lacy?"

"They'll be here," Hal said as he stroked Hope's cheek.

"Lacy's sick," Rex reminded him. "So we might end up getting married without Earl, Dane, or Lacy, and that would suck."

Hal kissed Hope's jaw and mumbled something that Rex couldn't hear. "Trust me, Rex. They'll show up. I best be on my way so Max doesn't leave without me."

"Dad, Ross is coming over to check out Hope this afternoon," Rex said.

Hal waved him off. "Hope'll be fine, too. She just needs you and Jade to work all this crap out."

Rex watched him walk up the hill and sidled up to Treat. "Dad still thinks he can talk to Mom through Hope. Should we be worried?"

Treat shook his head. "If you're worried about his mental faculties, no, you shouldn't worry. He's as sane as they get. If you're worried about whether he's going to fall apart if Hope dies…" He shrugged. "Won't we all?"

Chapter Five

JADE WATCHED THE nurse take her father's temperature and check his monitors and leads while Earl asked her four times when he could go home. The staff at Weston Memorial Hospital were efficient and compassionate, and Ben had already been by twice this morning. Jade had asked Ben about dietary restrictions for her father, and she took copious notes for her mother, who had been vacillating between acting perfectly fine and looking as if she were in a daze. Jade was as worried about her as she was about her father.

"Knock, knock," Max said as she came into the room with Hal. Max hugged Jane. "How're you holding up?"

"I'm okay, but Earl is ready to jump out of this bed." Jane squeezed Earl's arm.

"I'm sure he is." Max leaned down and kissed Earl's cheek. "You're ready to break out of this joint, Earl? Nothing can hold you down." Earl wasn't used to a sedentary lifestyle. He had retired from his agricultural engineering job a few years earlier. He'd been running the family ranch while working full-time, which meant that he now worked one job instead of two.

"Nice to see you, Max. I'm ready to get out of here, but Benji's keeping me for another day of observation. I'm waiting for them to take this damn pacemaker off of me so I can walk around. And by that I mean hightail it out of here. I swear he's just keeping me here to piss me off," Earl grumbled.

"Which is probably why he's keeping it on," Max said.

Earl grumbled something indiscernible in response. His eyes brightened when he greeted Hal. "Hal, nice of you to come by again," Earl said.

"Someone had to see if you were still faking all this crap," Hal kidded.

"Hey, at least I know how to have a *real* heart attack." A few years earlier Hal had suffered a case of broken heart syndrome, the symptoms of which mimic those of a heart attack. It was well before he and Earl had gotten over their feud, but it had become the brunt of a few running jokes, and Jade could tell that Hal took no offense to her father's comment.

"None of that broken heart syndrome shit for me. That's for sissies." Earl let out a deep laugh, then abruptly silenced. He flattened his hand against his chest and groaned.

Jane's eye went wide. "Earl? What is it? Jade, get Ben."

Jade was already heading for the door when her father's gruff command stopped her.

"I'm fine. Stay put, Jade."

"Dad?"

"It's normal for me to have a little chest pain. Didn't you two listen to anything that boy told us? Now get back in here and settle down, darlin'." Earl narrowed his eyes at Hal. A silent kinship passed between the two men.

"Eh, leave the old man alone," Hal said. "He knows what's going on in his own body."

"But he doesn't always respect it," Jade said. "I'm going to grab a cup of coffee and give you some privacy. Would anyone like some?"

"I'll come with you," Max offered. "Jane, would you like to come with us?"

Earl patted his wife's hand. "Please go, Janie. You've been here all day. Go enjoy a hen party."

"Dad!" Jade was relieved to see the tension in his face disappear and a smile curve his lips. "Come on, Mom." Jade linked arms with Max and her mother, and they headed down to the cafeteria just like that. A chain of strength.

"Before I forget, Max, can you give Mom your recipes for heart-healthy cooking?" Jade asked.

Max raised her brows. "You mean my secrets? Absolutely."

"Thank you, Max. If Earl knew I was making substitutions, he'd complain before he even tasted the food."

"Hal, too. Shh. Don't tell Treat, but I do it with him, too." Max and Jane laughed.

Jane put an arm around Jade. "How are you really holding up, baby girl?"

Jade sighed. "Okay, I guess. I just hope Ben is right and Dad will be okay. Even if he can't walk me down the aisle."

"Oh, he will walk you down that aisle, Jade. He dreamed of that day long before you ever did, and you know your father. He's a stubborn man."

Jade stepped into the elevator behind Max and her mother.

"So you don't think I'm doing the wrong thing by not postponing the wedding?"

The elevator doors opened, and they walked toward the cafeteria.

"I don't know, Jade. Your father thinks you shouldn't postpone it, so who are we to argue?" Her mother smiled, but Jade could see that she was as conflicted as Jade was.

"Rex isn't happy about not postponing."

"But he loves you so much, Jade. He'll do what you want to do," Max said. "I swear I've never seen such a brawny man soften when he talks about a woman the way Rex does when he talks about you."

"Except when Treat talks about you—or any of his brothers talk about their significant others," Jade reminded her.

"Maybe, but Treat's demeanor is gentler to start with. Rex is like this big brooding hulk, except when it comes to you, he's like a big teddy bear. Like Hal."

Jade's eyes welled with tears, and she stepped to the side of the hall. "God, I hate this. I'm sorry. I'm so emotional right now."

Jane put her arm around her. "It's okay, honey. We're *all* emotional right now. You'll feel better when your father's at home and out of that awful hospital gown. It makes him look fragile."

"Maybe," Jade said. "I'm sorry, Mom. I should be strong for you, and here I am as weepy as can be."

"It's okay, honey. We all cope differently, and you have a lot on your plate right now." She smiled, and it softened the worry lines on her forehead.

"Is there anything I can do to help?" Max asked.

Jade's phone rang, and she dug it out of her pocket. "It's Riley. Hold on a sec." She held the phone up to her ear. "Hi, Ri."

"Hey, how are you today?"

"Okay. Mom and Max are here at the hospital. Hal's in with Dad, so we're going down to the cafeteria."

"Josh and I get in tomorrow. I'll come straight over."

"I'm okay, really. It's just that everything feels like it's happening at once. I haven't found the necklace yet, and I'm afraid to leave Dad to go look for it."

"I know you'll find it," Riley said. "Those things have a way of popping up in the weirdest places."

"I hope you're right. Despite what Rex says, I don't know if he'd ever forgive me if it were lost forever."

REX PICKED UP feed, fixed a stall in the barn, and finished his afternoon chores at the ranch. Then he called the caterer, photographer, and the florist. Everything seemed in order for Sunday. Rex wasn't worried about the aspects of the wedding coming together, but he was worried about Jade. And he was worried about Earl and Hope. Not to mention that he wasn't sure he wanted to get married without his whole family there, which meant that if Dane and Lacy couldn't make it, he had another issue to consider. But every time he thought about pushing Jade to postpone the wedding, the hope in her eyes stopped him cold.

He'd received a text from Savannah confirming that she and her husband, Jack Remington, were arriving late tonight. He called his youngest brother, Hugh, to make sure he was still coming into town. With Earl, Hope, and Lacy falling ill, he was beginning to wonder if Jade had been right that losing the necklace was an omen. Was it? Should he push Jade harder to postpone the wedding?

Hugh answered on the second ring. "Hey, big brother."

"How's it hanging?" Rex smiled, because he knew what Hugh's response would be. Hugh was a successful race-car driver, and he'd been a smart-ass since the day he learned to speak. He had been a major player before meeting and marrying Brianna Heart, a single mother. Hugh had fallen head over heels for her and her daughter, Layla. Hugh had adopted Layla, and last year Brianna gave birth to their son, Christian.

"Longer than yours." Hugh laughed. "Getting prewedding jitters yet?"

"Who are you kidding? I'd run down that aisle to marry Jade, but her father's in the hospital, so things are a little up in the air."

"Aw, man. I'm sorry. I had no idea. I've been out of touch for the last two days. We've been on the road, coming back from my race down in Florida."

"I heard you won. Congrats."

"Don't I always?" Hugh smirked. "But seriously, how is Earl? How's Jade holding up? She's a daddy's girl at heart, even though she puts up a strong front."

"Yeah, she is. She's worried. Ben said Earl should be released from the hospital on Saturday, but Jade and Earl won't let me postpone the wedding."

He paced the yard, thinking about Jade. Damn it, he'd forgotten to look for the necklace.

"And we can't find her Dance of Two Lovers necklace, so she's stressed about that, too. Hope's not doing well, and Jade's convinced that her father and Hope are somehow tied to losing the necklace. That it's some kind of sign."

"Shit, Rex. Sounds like all hell's breaking loose down there. We're arriving tomorrow morning. I'll do whatever I can to help."

"Thanks, Hugh. Have you talked to Dane?"

"Yeah. I heard Lacy's sick."

"I know. I wish Jade would let me postpone the damn wedding."

"Relax. Don't make any decisions yet. See how things pan out tomorrow. What's the worst that can happen? We'll all spend a weekend together and you'll still be single," Hugh taunted.

"That would totally suck. You get that, right?"

"Hey, look who you're talking to. I would have married Brianna two days after meeting her if I could have. I don't know how you lasted four years without marrying Jade."

Hugh offered to fly in tonight instead of tomorrow, but Rex told him it wasn't necessary. They talked about Hope and their father, and after they ended the call, Rex wanted to hear Jade's voice and make sure she was okay. She answered on the second ring.

"Hi," Jade answered.

"Hey, babe. How's your dad?"

"He's arguing with Ben at the moment. I think he's feeling better."

Rex let out a relieved sigh. "Thank goodness. And how are you and your mom doing?"

"Mom's good. She's much better now that Dad's feistier, and I'm okay, I guess. I hate seeing him in the hospital, but at least it looks like he'll be okay for the wedding."

Rex closed his eyes for a beat, hearing his father's words sail through his mind. *There are times in every father's life when he has to step in and do the thinking for his children.* "Your father really wants this to happen."

"I know. Please don't ask me again to postpone the wedding. I'm sick of being questioned."

"What am I supposed to do, Jade? Sit back and pretend that this is all okay? That I'm excited to talk to the florist and photographer while your father's lying in the hospital and Hope is getting sicker by the minute?"

"I don't know."

"Well, I wish someone did." Rex looked up at the sound of tires on gravel. Damn it. He hadn't called her to argue. He wanted to drive straight to the hospital, take Jade in his arms, and smooth all this shit over—but there was no time for that now. "I've got to go. Ross just showed up."

He pushed to his feet to greet his cousin. Ross was one of Hal's sister Catherine's children. He had five siblings, and they had been raised by their single mother after their father had taken off with another woman.

Ross stepped from his truck with a leather medical bag in his hand. "Sorry I'm late, Rex. It was a busy day."

"That's all right. I'm glad you could make it." He embraced his tall, dark cousin. Ross was more reserved than his rambunctious siblings and reminded Rex of his brother Josh, also the most reserved of their family.

"Let's take a look at old Hope." Ross headed toward the barn. "My mother talked to Uncle Hal last night and said Earl's in the hospital. How's Jade holding up?"

"She's doing okay."

"I assume you're delaying the wedding?"

Rex shook his head as they walked into the barn. "Earl and Jade won't hear of it."

"Well, then, Earl's prognosis must be good." Ross stepped into the stall with Hope. "How's it going, girl?"

When Hope didn't lift her head to greet him, as she normally did, Ross said, "She's definitely not herself, is she? Has she been eating?"

"On and off, but definitely not like she usually does."

"Has anything else changed? Exercise patterns? Do you still ride her daily?"

"Actually, no. I stopped riding her about two weeks ago. She's getting old, and I was worried about wearing her out." Rex thought back to when he'd made the decision. His father had fought him on it. He'd wanted Rex to continue taking their morning rides, at least on Sundays, which was the one day of the week Rex had never missed riding Hope.

"Did Hope's behavior change at all then?" Ross took Hope's temperature, listened to her breathing and to her gut sounds. He checked her teeth and gums and did a skin-pinch test, checking for dehydration.

"I can't remember her seeming so sullen, but then again, things were pretty busy around that same time. Jade and I were running around getting final wedding details situated, and..." Rex took off his hat and scrubbed his hand down his face. "I don't know. I wasn't paying close enough attention." *And I hate myself for it.*

"Don't beat yourself up over it." Ross checked Hope's pulse and her joints and eyes while Rex paced.

"Is Jade still doing massage on Hope? I asked Elisabeth, but she said Jade's been so busy with the wedding that she wasn't sure." Ross's fiancée, Elisabeth, referred clients to Jade and vice versa. When Elisabeth had moved to Trusty to take over her aunt's pie-making business, she had also opened a pet-pampering business, and Jade had helped her get her business off the ground.

"She's been a little overwhelmed these last few weeks, too." Ross stroked Hope's jaw. "Horses are a lot like people, as you know. And I can't find a darn thing wrong with Hope. I think there's a good chance she's depressed. You've changed the riding schedule she's had for years, and if Jade has changed her massage schedule, too, well, Hope might just be feeling lonely."

"Depressed? Well, I'll be damned. My father said she wanted me and Jade to work through this wedding stuff." He let out a low laugh. "I was almost starting to believe him." *Depressed.* Rex felt guilty as hell. He loved Hope with the same vehemence as the rest of his family did, and to think that he'd caused her pain by changing her schedule cut him to his core.

"You should consider taking her out on a ride and having Jade do some massage, and see if you notice any behavioral changes. If not, I'll come back out, but her vitals are good, and she doesn't show any signs of discomfort. Don't let her age be your guide to her exercise. Every horse is different. I know you know that, and I know you take particular care with Hope because of your mom. But don't forget that some horses can be ridden right up until they're almost ready to leave us."

"I didn't make the decision lightly. I thought I was protecting her from injury."

"Most ranchers do." Ross patted his shoulder. "You've had a lot on your plate, Rex. Just love her up like you always have, and see if that does the trick. If she does well, then just be sure someone rides her while you and Jade are on your honeymoon."

"We're not taking one right away." Rex shrugged. "Neither of us is aching to get off the ranch. Treat and Pierce both offered us a free stay at a resort of our choice, but there's no place calling to us at the moment." Pierce was Ross's eldest brother, and he owned several casinos and resorts.

"I understand that. Elisabeth and I are the same way."

"Thanks for coming out, Ross."

"You'll let me know if the wedding is postponed?" Ross headed for his truck.

"Yeah, of course. I'm relieved that you didn't find something terribly wrong with Hope. Not that depression is minor, but you know. It's better than finding out I have to tell Dad she's on her way out."

Ross set his bag in the truck. "When that day comes, it'll be Hal we're monitoring for depression."

"When that day comes, I think you'll be monitoring more than just one Braden."

Chapter Six

"MOM, GO HOME and get some rest. I'll stay with Dad."
Jade had been trying to convince her mother to go home for the
past two hours. It was late and Jade was cranky. Seeing her
mother hovering over her father made her even edgier. Friends
had been in and out, visiting her father all day, and every
countertop in his room was covered with vases and get-well
cards. She didn't mind answering questions about her father,
but she was tired of answering questions about her wedding.
She didn't even know if she was doing the right thing by having
the wedding on Sunday. She hoped she was, and her father
seemed determined that she and Rex get married. Jade did her
best to be accommodating, but she was also stressed over Hope,
and despite what Rex had said that morning, she couldn't shake
the feeling that she'd really screwed up by losing the necklace.
While her father was visiting with friends, she'd called every
client she'd visited over the past two weeks, but no one had
found it.

She felt like she was dog-paddling in the middle of the sea
and wished someone would throw her a life raft with all the
answers on it. They'd unhooked her father's pacemaker and
were monitoring him through tomorrow afternoon, and then,

finally, he'd go home. Ben had assured her multiple times that all indications were good for her father to be released tomorrow. Her father had already taken a short walk down the hall. He'd seemed fine afterward, and Ben was pleased with his progress. That had to mean something.

Jade wanted to go home and make up for the way her call had ended with Rex, but she didn't want to leave her father's side until a few hours had passed so she knew he was really out of the woods without the pacemaker. Her father wasn't much of a talker, and with her mother going in and out of her zombie-like state, Jade had way too much quiet time to sit and stew over the last few days and her impending wedding. The hospital smelled sterile, which she hadn't really noticed the day before. She'd been too upset to notice much of anything, but now the smell was an annoying reminder of her father's heart attack. But if her father had to be there, she felt compelled to be there, too.

Her brother had come and gone earlier in the day, and now if she could just convince her mother to go home and rest, she'd stay a while longer and then go home and get some rest herself. How long she'd stay, she wasn't sure. She didn't have a magic time frame in mind. Maybe her father would go to sleep and then she'd know he was okay. She couldn't even think clearly.

"Jade's right, sweet pea. Go home and get some rest. To-morrow's our big day. Benji said I should be out of here by two." Her father touched her mother's cheek. Jane covered his hand with hers and smiled.

The love between her parents was as real as the love between her and Rex. She took comfort in seeing her father soothe her mother's worry. It made him seem less fragile and more like the protector he'd always been.

"Okay, Earl, but make sure Jade goes home soon, too. She

has a wedding to prepare for."

Jade hugged her mother goodbye and promised not to stay too late. After her mother left, Jade asked her father if he needed anything.

"No thank you, darlin'. Come sit over here with me." He patted the side of the bed.

She settled in beside him. Up close the fine lines around his eyes and mouth were more prominent, but his eyes hadn't changed. There was strength in his gaze—as there had been Jade's whole life. She took comfort in that, too.

"I don't want you to worry about your old man. I'm going to be just fine. You should go on home and get some rest."

"I will soon." Jade hadn't told her father about the necklace, and damn it, maybe it was selfish, but she needed to hear from the man who always seemed to know right from wrong—except where that darn feud was concerned—that things would be okay.

Tears welled in her eyes as she confessed what had been weighing heavily on her heart. "Dad, I lost the necklace Rex's mom left for him."

Her father's eyes filled with compassion. "No wonder you've been so sad lately."

"That's because of your heart attack," Jade said.

Her father held her hand and smiled up at her. It was the first real smile she'd seen since he'd landed in the hospital. "Darlin', let me tell you a little something. You know how your mother and Rex's mother used to sneak out and get the kids together when they thought Hal and I were too busy to notice?"

"When the two of you were feuding, sure. Mom told me about it."

"Well, there are certain things a person just knows. The way you know you love Rex and the way Steven knows he belongs in the mountains. I knew your mama was out there keeping the two families tethered together by some thin connection, and I'd bet that Hal did, too. Although he's as stubborn as a mule and would probably never admit it."

He shook his head. "Hal and I might have been feuding, but the loss we all felt when his wife died didn't go away with the tincture of time. I know it didn't for your mother, and you have seen that Hal still believes he can communicate with her."

"Through Hope." She had caught Hal talking to Hope like she was Adriana at least a dozen times over the years.

"Right. Crazy old bastard." His smile told Jade he didn't believe Hal was either of those things. "Anyway, the bond between Rex and his mother isn't there because of the necklace. It's in his heart, darlin'. That won't go away because you lost a necklace."

"But the way it came to us after all those years. Dad, we walked into that shop, Jewels of the Past, in Allure—thirty or more miles from here—and that woman somehow *knew* it was meant for us. If that's not a miracle, then I don't know what is."

Earl sighed. "So you believe there was some greater force behind that piece of jewelry?"

"I think so, yes. It's too strange to be anything else. I know it sounds crazy, but it doesn't feel crazy. And that day we walked into the shop, it didn't feel crazy either. Everything felt right. Our love magnified. I wish you could have seen how the necklace impacted Rex. He had a full-on panic attack, and it was like everything came together at once. Our hearts, our love...our lives. Daddy, I hate that I lost the one thing that meant something to him."

"You didn't."

Jade spun around at the sound of Rex's voice. Rex came to her side and reached for her hand. "Hi, baby." He lifted his eyes to Earl. "Earl, are you feeling okay?"

"I am, Rex. Thank you."

"Then would you mind if I borrowed my future wife for a moment?"

"Please." Earl shooed her off the bed. "She won't leave my side."

"What are you doing here?" Jade asked as Rex led her out of the hospital room and down the hall.

"You wouldn't come home, and I didn't want to be there without you." He pushed open a hospital room door, and Jade gasped at the sight of a candlelit dinner set up in the far end of the room.

"Rex?"

"I pulled a few strings so we could have some privacy. I promised them we wouldn't be longer than thirty minutes— and that they wouldn't have to change the sheets. You didn't lose the one thing that meant something to me. You're right here, Jade." His mouth met hers in a tender kiss. "I love you. I'm so sorry for snapping at you earlier."

"Me too. I've been upset all evening."

He lifted her in his arms, and her legs naturally wrapped around his waist as he took her in a deep, soulful kiss that eased the pain in her heart. He turned them so Jade's back was against the wall and pressed his body to hers.

"You feel amazing. I should marry you," Rex teased.

"You're not mad about not postponing the wedding?"

He kissed her again. "I was never mad. I worry that you'll be disappointed if your father can't walk you down the aisle. I love you so damn much, Jade. All I have ever wanted was to make you happy."

She lowered her mouth to the swatch of skin and peppering of chest hair exposed by his open neckline and kissed her way around the base of his neck.

"I can think of one way you can make me very happy," she whispered.

A deep groan rumbled through his chest. "No changing the sheets, remember?"

"Oh, yeah." She pressed her lips to his. "Guess I'll have to be happy with this."

Rex carried her while they kissed, and sat down on a chair with her straddling his lap.

His eager length was hard beneath her. She was damp and was tempted to taunt him into taking her right there and then. She wanted to be closer to him, to feel him inside her. To borrow his strength and soak up his love.

He deepened the kiss, then drew back, brushing his lips over her cheek. "If we're getting married on Sunday, then you're going to be Jade Johnson for only one more day, and I want to kiss you as much as I can between now and then. The rest can wait."

He kissed her again, a slow, torturous, teasing kiss that left her craving more, and whispered, "Maybe."

Chapter Seven

SATURDAY MORNING JADE got up early and went down
to the barn to massage Hope before going to help her mother
take her father home from the hospital. Jade had been too tired
to move when Rex got up at four thirty, but now, at seven, she
was ready for the day and excited that her father was coming
home. She walked through the woods between their property
and Hal's instead of driving. It was a beautiful morning,
mirroring the hope in Jade's heart. Streaks of sunshine peeked
through the woods, illuminating the trail before her. She loved
these peaceful moments when she could hear squirrels scamper-
ing across leaves and birds singing in the trees. The last few days
had been so chaotic that she and Rex hadn't shared much
downtime, but last night had rejuvenated her.

She thought of the glint in his eyes when he was getting
ready to go ride Hope this morning. Rex needed that ride as
much as Hope did—Jade was sure of it. She smiled at the
thought as she came to the edge of Hal's property and stepped
free of the woods. Acres of pastures spread out before her,
anchored by barns and Rex's childhood home. How many years
had she ridden her horse by that ranch hoping to catch a
glimpse of Rex? She'd loved Rex for as long as she could

remember, but because of the feud between their fathers, she'd never dreamed he'd give her a second look—much less that they'd ever have a chance at being together. That's why she'd gone away to Oklahoma for school. It had been too hard having her heart long for a man she'd never have.

Only now she had him.

And now that her father was coming home from the hospital, she could breathe a little easier and revel in the family barbecue they had planned for their last night as an engaged couple.

She wasn't surprised to find Rex, Savannah, and Jack in the barn with Hope. Savannah and Jack lived in New York and had a cabin in the Colorado Mountains. They'd married on Hal's ranch last year, and Savannah was four months pregnant.

"Jade!" Savannah's green eyes widened with her smile as she threw her arms around Jade. "I just heard that your dad's coming home today. That's wonderful news."

"Yeah, we're all feeling pretty good about tomorrow." Jade touched Savannah's auburn hair, which she'd cut to just below her shoulders. "I love your new cut." She patted Savannah's belly. "And your baby bump."

"Thanks. I can't believe in a few months we'll actually meet our baby."

Jack embraced Jade. "How're you doing, sweetie?" He was a burly man, like Rex, with a body as hard as stone and a heart as soft as cotton. He'd lost his first wife in a car accident two years before meeting Savannah. Savannah's love had helped him heal.

"It's been a rough few days, but I think we're all much better now. Thanks for asking."

Rex pulled her in close and pressed his lips to hers.

"Oh, here we go," Savannah teased. "Okay, lover boy. Save

it for the wedding night."

Rex laughed. "Come on, Jack. Let's go hang with Treat and Dad."

Rex kissed Jade again and held her hand, slowly taking a step away until all that touched were their fingertips. "Love you, babe."

"Love you, too, Rexy."

"Come on. You're making me look bad." Jack tugged Rex up the hill.

"You two are still so cute, it kills me." Savannah stroked Hope's side.

"So are you guys." Hope pressed her head to Jade's chest. "Hi, Hope. I'm sorry I've been sidetracked, but I'm focused now, and I'll love you up. I promise."

"Do you mind if I watch?" Savannah grabbed a blanket from the stall behind her and tossed it on the ground, then sat cross-legged on it.

Jade walked around to Hope's side and pressed her hands flat against her warm coat. "Not at all."

Jade closed her eyes, centering her mind on Hope. She worked her hands along Hope's shoulder in long, slow strokes, easing the tension from her muscles. She concentrated on Hope's shoulder and made her way down Hope's front leg. As she kneaded and soothed, Jade instinctively felt for tender spots, completely in tune with Hope's reactions. She worked her way across Hope's chest muscles and the points of her shoulders, then concentrated on her shoulder again before moving to her back. Jade reveled in being close to Hope again. She'd missed this connection to Hope, and as she moved across Hope's loins and hindquarters, first with her hands splayed, then jostling Hope slightly, loosening and lengthening the muscles, she remembered the first time she'd taken her hands to Rex. He'd been as tense as any horse she'd ever touched, but he'd eventually melted beneath her touch, the way she'd softened to his every day since.

"Watching you is like watching some sort of weird horse and girl porn," Savannah said.

Jade smiled. She'd been in the zone and had forgotten Savannah was watching.

"I bet Rex loves that."

"You hate when I talk about sexy things and your brother."

"Yeah." Savannah sighed. "But I can see Rex needing massages like this. He's so bottled up all the time."

"Not with me." Jade went to work on Hope's other side, stopping to kiss Hope's head along the way.

"I know. With you he's like a gentle giant, but with everyone else, he's this hulking, brooding creature," Savannah said. "Hope looks like she's enjoying the massage."

"She is. I can feel it." Jade worked her hands along Hope's neck. "I'll never put off another massage—I promise you that."

"You've been busy with your dad and the wedding. I can't imagine how you're holding it together with everything that's going on." Savannah came around Hope and stood beside Jade. "What do you make of my family's connection to Hope and...?"

"And your mom?" Jade asked.

Savannah nodded.

"I think love works in strange ways. Your mother's love for you guys was obviously so powerful that it's impacted each one of your lives in a different way. Look at me and Rex." Her heart ached just thinking about the necklace she'd lost.

"For the woman who owned Jewels of the Past to *know* that

necklace from your mom was meant for us?" Jade had always believed that there were bigger forces at play with the way the necklace came to them. "That's the power I'm talking about. And the way your father loves this horse and talks to your mom when he's down here…How can that *not* be real? I wish your mom were alive to see us get married. To see you all get married, really. But I think she's with us in spirit."

Savannah touched Hope's neck, and Hope turned her big head toward her. "I just hope I can be half the mother mine was. I don't remember her well, but my brothers have filled my head with so many loving memories that I can imagine what she was like and I want to emulate that love with our children."

"You are going to be an amazing mother. Everything you do emulates love. Love is in the way you look at Jack. The way you touch his hand. The way you tease your brothers, and even in the way you get excited every time you see me or Brianna, Max, Lacy, or Riley. Love just is, and you're full of it."

"Thanks, Jade. I hope you're right."

Jade spotted Rex and Jack heading back down toward the barn with Treat. Jack was carrying Dylan and Rex was holding Adriana's hand. "Look at our men. Have you ever seen a more beautiful sight?"

"Never."

Jade sighed, feeling so full of love that she was near tears again. "All I know is that when you love someone as much as I love Rex and you love Jack, there's no hope involved. Love just is."

Chapter Eight

THERE WAS LITTLE on this earth more important than family to Rex, and as he looked around the tables they'd set up in Hal's side yard for the family barbeque Saturday evening, his heart felt as if it were going to burst. Earl and Hal were sitting side by side, two hulking men with wide smiles, laughing heartily at something Rex hadn't heard. Jade's mother sat beside Earl, filling his plate with greens. Jade, Riley, and Savannah were whispering to one another while Jack and Hugh carried steaks and hamburgers from the stone grill where Josh was cooking and set them on the table. Brianna bounced Christian on her knee as he gnawed on a toy, and Layla and Adriana were spinning circles in the grass and giggling. Shannon was sitting with Steve. She tucked her dark hair behind her ear and smiled. It was a flirtatious, shy smile. The kind that had Rex looking more closely at Steve. There was no mistaking the interest in his eyes. He took a step closer, and Treat looked up from where he sat on one side of Dylan's high chair. Max sat on Dylan's other side. Treat lifted his chin and smiled at Rex, a silent understanding of the wonder of family and love passing between them.

Rex joined Josh at the grill instead of coming between his cousin and Steve. Who was he to get involved? He couldn't help how protective he was, but Steve was a good guy, and surely Shannon could handle herself. She'd grown up with a handful of older brothers, too.

"You doing okay, big brother?" Josh nudged Rex's shoulder. Their family events always revolved around a barbecue, and sometime over the years, Josh had become the cook. After tomorrow he and Dane would be the last two unmarried Braden men in their family, though both were engaged.

"I'm better than okay now that Jade's father is home. I was worried for a while there. But I wish I could reach Dane and Lacy. I'm worried about her."

"If something had gone really wrong, or if she took a turn for the worse, Dane would have called us. You know that. I know they had an appointment with a doctor. He probably turned the phones off so Lacy could rest or something."

Josh and Riley had arrived as dinner was getting started, and Josh had come directly down to the barbecue. Rex eyed his brother's suit coat and tie. "Why are you still all dolled up?"

Unlike Rex, whose body was homegrown from years of hard physical labor, of which his bulging muscles gave proof, Josh was two hundred pounds of sleek, well-defined muscles from long runs in New York City. As a world-renowned fashion designer, Josh wore clothing tailored to his tall, lean body to perfection. Luckily, while his clothing and career might have taken a highfalutin turn, Josh hadn't forgotten his roots. He still had a down-to-earth, country-boy personality that kept him grounded.

"No freaking idea." Josh took off his suit coat and tie and laid them over the back of a chair. "You know, now that you're tying the knot, Riley and I can't put our wedding off any longer."

"No shit. You guys keep waiting for your schedules to ease up. Waiting for the perfect time." Rex glanced at Earl. "If I've learned one thing from this, it's that perfect doesn't exist. Marry her, Josh. Stop waiting and start your life."

Josh's gaze shifted to Riley. "We're ready to start a family, so we've got to check off the marriage box."

"Me too, man. Me too."

Josh put the last of the meat and potatoes on plates, and they carried them to the table. Josh sat beside Riley, who immediately reached for his hand, and Rex sat beside Jade.

Jade leaned in close and whispered, "You're the most handsome man here."

"You're a little biased." He kissed her softly. "But I like your bias."

Treat tapped his spoon on his glass and rose to his feet. "I'd like to say a few words."

"Of course you would," Hugh teased.

"I was going to start by saying something about you winning your most recent race, you wiseass," Treat said.

Josh and Rex picked up their glasses and said, "To *Huge*."

The men laughed at the nickname.

Savannah rolled her eyes. "You guys! You're not teenagers anymore."

The men passed serious looks between one another, then burst out laughing again.

"Vanny, since when does that matter?" Treat asked.

"I don't know," Savannah said. "Shouldn't you act your age? We've got kids at the table now. You're role models."

That caused even more laughter.

"Settle down now, boys." Hal rose to his feet. "Savannah has a point. We wouldn't want to be a bad influence on the next generation of Bradens." He looked at Jack and Savannah. "Or Remingtons. They might just turn out like y'all did." He set a hand on Earl's shoulder. "Or worse, like me and Earl."

Earl smiled up at him.

Hal nodded toward Layla and Adriana playing in the grass. "That's what growing up is all about. Enjoying the moments. Those girls aren't worried about Uncle Hugh's ridiculous nickname—"

"Hey, I live up to that nickname." Huge pulled Brianna in close and kissed her temple. "Don't I, babe?"

Brianna smiled as he pressed his lips to hers.

"As I was saying," Hal continued. "They're not worried about nicknames. I would worry if we *didn't* have them. What we have around this table is flat-out love, and plenty of it." Hal sat back down and nodded to Treat.

"Well, there you have it. I think I'll skip my speech and go straight to the only thing that matters." Treat raised his glass. "To family."

Rex touched his forehead to Jade's. "To family," he whispered. "Yours, mine, and—one day—ours."

Chapter Nine

SUNDAY MORNING REX awoke to a whisper across his skin and his mother's voice in his ear.

Dress.

One word, a word he couldn't make heads or tails of. *Dress?* He went through a litany of words that sounded the same as *dress*, but still came up blank.

He lay awake in the predawn hours thinking about how he felt like they were finally out of the woods. Having his family together again, save for Dane and Lacy, with Earl getting healthier by the hour, and about to marry the woman of his dreams, Rex felt rejuvenated. He dressed and headed to his father's ranch, excited to take Hope out for a ride.

His boots were damp with dew by the time he trekked through the last of the thick grass to the barn. He opened the heavy barn doors, and as if she'd been waiting for him, Hope neighed. He saddled her up, thinking about the first of his Sunday-morning rides with Hope. He'd been just eight years old, the Sunday after his mother had passed away. Even after all these years, he wasn't positive what had startled him awake on that very first Sunday after she'd passed, but he swore it was his mother's whispering voice that had led him down to the barn and had him mounting Hope. He assumed it was, as he'd heard her whisper several times in the years since, just as he had earlier that morning.

Dress.

He didn't know what it meant, but like all other things that seemed to come from his mother, he accepted that one day he would.

He rode Hope along the familiar trail that bordered his property on one side and his father's on the other. Hope knew just where to turn. They'd been riding these trails for thirty years, and Hope guided Rex more than Rex needed to guide Hope. She followed the windy trail toward the ravine where Rex and Jade had first seen each other after Jade had moved back into town to start her veterinary practice. Rex remembered the brisk morning when fate had brought them together. When he'd first seen her four years ago, standing by the water, her stallion, Flame, standing off to the side with a bum leg, fifteen years of unrequited desire reared up, and he'd debated turning around and leaving before she'd spotted him, but he'd been drawn to her like a moth to flame.

He still was.

Hope walked south on the hill above Devil's Bend, where the ravine curved at a sharp angle and the water pooled before dropping twenty feet into a bed of rocks. It had been there where he'd seen Jade. He remembered the cream-colored T-shirt she'd worn, the way it had hugged her curves and contrasted sharply against her jet-black, waist-length hair. She'd been stunning then, and she'd only grown more beautiful over recent years. Rex petted Hope's mane.

"You guided me here then, too, Hope."

Hope neighed and nodded her big head up and down. Not

for the first time—and he was sure it wouldn't be the last—Rex thought about how connected Hope was to their family, and more specifically, to him. Their rides had pulled him through the awful weeks after his mother's death and the frustrated years when he was in love with Jade and unable to let it be known because of his loyalty to his father and his father's asinine feud with the Johnsons. He'd ridden Hope over to Jade's house when they'd first started dating, and she'd guided him, unbidden, back to Jade too many times since to count. He didn't know what the bottom line was with Hope or her connection to his mother. Maybe it was in all of their heads and they saw and heard what they wanted to or needed to. But he did believe that it was fate that had led him and Jade into Jewels of the Past. What he'd felt the day they'd walked in and the moment he'd seen that necklace and the way his father had reacted to the necklace afterward told him that he and Jade were meant to love each other—and somehow his mother had known that before he'd even been born.

He rode Hope back to the barn. His brothers were outside setting up the yard for the wedding. He'd spent the last few days worrying for nothing. Jade would have her wedding. Her father would give her away, and they'd be united on the ground where he was raised. He was a lucky man. Not only did he have the most caring family he could ever wish for, but today he was marrying the woman he'd loved his whole life. Rex knew that if Dane didn't make it to the wedding, he was thinking of them, just like he believed his mother was. Wherever she may be.

JADE SAT ON her bed with the phone pressed to her ear.

She'd called to check on her father and was relieved to hear he was doing well. He had even taken a walk after lunch, and now, hours later, was relaxing on the porch with Steve.

"Thanks, Mom. Steve said he was bringing you and Dad over. I love you, and I'll see you when you get here." Jade ended the call and tried to ignore the bees nesting in her stomach.

In an hour she was going to marry Rex. One hour. Sixty— oops—fifty minutes. *Less than an hour.* How did brides make it through the final hour? She wanted to put her dress on and drag Rex to the altar right now, but her old-fashioned husband-to-be had gone out with Hope at the break of dawn, and she wouldn't see him again until they were walking down the aisle. Never mind that he'd made sweet love to her that morning. Her hunky alpha cowboy lived by his own pick-and-choose old-fashioned values, and she loved him even more for it.

"Knock, knock." Riley's voice came from downstairs.

Jade jumped off her bed just in time for her best girlfriends to come to her rescue. She ran down the stairs and into the arms of Riley, Max, Savannah, and Brianna, all dressed in above-the-knee bridesmaid dresses. Riley had not only designed Jade's wedding gown, but she'd also designed simple strapless dresses with crisscross bodices that the girls could wear on any number of occasions.

"You're here!" she squealed. "You all look gorgeous."

"Of course we're here," Riley said. "Shannon said to tell you she hoped you would be okay with her helping with the babies while we helped you get ready. She said she never gets any baby time."

"She's such a doll. Of course I don't mind."

"So…" Riley raised her brows in quick succession. "Did you guys have a *nice* night?"

"We had a hot, sexy night." Jade bumped her hip against Riley's.

"Ew! That's my brother, remember?" Savannah dragged Jade over to the couch. "Sit down. We're going to make you beautiful."

"What?" Jade said. "No. Thank you, but you guys know that kind of stuff drives me nutty. I'm going to wear my hair down, the way Rex likes it. I can't wait to see him all dressed up. He's going to look so hot in his black vest, with all those beautiful muscles packed into that white dress shirt, and topped off with his Stetson. I swear he's the hottest cowboy that ever lived."

"Yeah, yeah, he's pretty handsome." Savannah sighed. "Fine, no hair stuff. Let's at least do a few shots to get rid of the jitters, because you are incredibly uptight."

"Am I? Oh God. Can you really tell?" She followed the girls into the kitchen.

"Are you worried about your dad?" Max asked as she took glasses out of the cabinet.

"Not really. I just talked to Mom and he feels good. I think we're okay. I just wish I could have found the Dance of Two Lovers necklace. I'll never get over losing that."

Savannah folded her in her arms. "Well, get over it, because that was a thing, not a person. And things aren't ever as important as the people they came from or the people they were meant for."

"Thanks, Savannah."

"So, when are you going to start a family?" Brianna asked. Jade knew she was trying to distract her from the necklace. "If you start right away there won't be a big age difference between yours and Savannah's babies." Brianna filled four shot glasses.

Jade waved her hand. "My cycle is so messed up. I think it'll take months to get it regular again after all this stress."

"*Tsk.*" Riley shook her head. "I've known you since we both got our first periods, and you've never been irregular in your life."

"Yeah, well, I think it's pretty normal to miss your period when you're under as much stress as I have been. I didn't even realize I had missed it until this morning."

The girls exchanged a knowing glance.

"Don't even go there, you guys. I am sure this is just stress." Jade's pulse quickened at the thought of being pregnant. It would be just her luck to get pregnant right before her wedding. She pushed the shot a few inches away.

"You told me that you stopped taking the pill a few months ago so you would be ready to start your family after the wedding," Riley reminded her.

"Yes, but we're supercareful," Jade insisted. "We use the rhythm method."

"Dylan's a rhythm baby," Max said with a wide smile.

"Oh my gosh, you guys. Stop it. I am *not* pregnant." She stalked out of the kitchen, feeling less sure with every step.

"You know what they call people who use the rhythm method?" Savannah asked.

"Parents," Brianna answered with a laugh. "Rex will be over the moon!"

"No, he won't. Marriage before babies, remember?" Jade sank down onto the couch. "And don't you dare say anything. We don't even know if I'm pregnant. Savannah, you know how your brother believes in weddings first, babies second."

Savannah sipped a glass of water. "That he does, but he also believes in fate."

"And this is totally fate," Riley added.

"Great. Thanks, you guys. Now I need to find out for sure.

I can't get married not knowing." Jade headed for the front door. "Where are my keys?"

"Wait. I have a pregnancy test at home," Max said.

"You do?" Jade asked.

"Of course. When I thought I was pregnant, I bought a few just in case." Max grabbed her purse. "I'll go get it. Stay here." Her dark hair flew behind her as she ran out the front door.

"This is so exciting!" Brianna said. "I have to call Lacy if you *are* pregnant. She'll want to know."

"And then we get to plan a baby shower," Savannah added.

"I can't be pregnant." Jade paced the living room. "I'm not pregnant. This is just stress. It has to be."

Riley draped an arm over her shoulder and lowered her voice. "Relax, Jade. If you are, you are. And if you're not, then your plans will stay on track. Rex loves you either way."

"But I'm not prepared. If I'm pregnant, shouldn't I have been taking prenatal vitamins? What if I am pregnant and I've already hurt the baby somehow?" She racked her brain thinking about what she'd done over the last few weeks. "Rex and I shared a bottle of wine last week."

"Our bodies are amazing vessels, Jade," Brianna said. "Some women don't know they're pregnant until they're five or six months along, and I'm sure lots of them have wine now and again. Is this your first missed period?"

"I think so." She was too overwhelmed to think straight.

While Savannah and Brianna planned Jade's baby's life, she and Riley sat on the couch waiting for Max.

"You know that if you are pregnant, it's okay, right, Jade? You're just freaking out because it's your wedding day."

"If you're asking if I'll be happy about a baby, yes. I'll be ecstatic, but..." Tears streamed down her cheeks. "I lost his necklace, and now if I'm pregnant, I messed that up, too."

"Oh Lord. I can tell you right now that you're pregnant. Forget the test, because you are *never* this emotional. I guess it could be because you're worried about your dad, too, but something tells me that this has to be pregnancy hormones."

"Riley! You're not helping," Jade snapped.

"I'm just being honest. Look at you. You're *weeping*, Jade. You never cry, much less weep." She put her arm around Jade and hugged her close. "You're so cute when you're pregnant."

"Stop it!"

Max flew through the front door with a little white box held over her head. "I've got it! Into the bathroom, ladies."

Jade headed for the bathroom. The girls hurried behind her. Savannah and Brianna giggled and whispered as they pushed through the bathroom door behind Max and Riley.

"Hey, can I just pee by myself?"

"Sorry," they mumbled as all except for Riley filed out.

Jade's jaw dropped open.

"Oh, come on. Really? I can't even stay?" Riley pleaded.

Jade pointed to the door. "Out. I love you, but I need a minute."

"Fine." Riley pouted and closed the door behind her.

Jade stared in the mirror. *Pregnant? No, this is just a mistake. It's stress.* She read the instructions on the box.

"Jade?" Max's voice came through the closed door.

"Did you do it yet?" Riley yelled.

"No. I'm thinking."

"Thinking is totally overrated. Pee on it already," Savannah said. "I want to know if I'm going to be an auntie or not."

"Fine. Gosh, you guys, go away from the door." Jade smiled despite her worries. She squatted over the stick and did her business, then set it on the counter and washed her hands.

She took a deep breath and opened the bathroom door.

Riley practically fell into the bathroom. Max, Savannah, and Brianna laughed as they stumbled over one another and piled in.

"Gosh, you guys." Jade shook her head. "You're like…"

"The best friends *ever*," Riley offered.

Jade's cell phone rang. She ran out to the coffee table and picked it up.

"Hi, Mom." Jade watched the girls hovering over the sink.

"Honey, we're back at the hospital."

Jade's hearing fogged over. She sank silently down to the couch as her mother explained.

"Your father had chest pains again, and we rushed him right over. They're checking him out now."

Daddy. She listened to her mother, and when she ended the call, she barely registered the girls yelling, "You're pregnant!"

REX WAS IN his father's bedroom, looking at a photograph of his parents, when Adriana walked in wearing a pretty pink dress.

"What are you doing, Uncle Rex?"

"Just looking at a picture of your grandma and grandpa when they were teenagers." He picked her up and set her on the bed beside him. "You look like a princess in that dress."

"Thank you. I've seen that picture before. That's Grandma Adriana. I'm named after her. Daddy said that other than Mommy and me, she was the most beautiful girl in the world."

"Your daddy was right, but I'd add Aunt Jade to that list, too."

Adriana blinked up at him through long, dark lashes. "Why do you look sad, Uncle Rex?"

"I'm not sad. Just thinking. See the necklace your grandma is wearing?" He pointed to the Dance of Two Lovers necklace around his mother's neck. "I think we lost it."

"Oh. I lost a necklace once and we found it in the dryer."

"The dryer. Hm. Now, that's one place I haven't looked." Rex kissed the top of Adriana's head.

"Before Mommy found my necklace, I was sad. Daddy said that it was just a thing, and that things don't fill our hearts— people do."

Rex had heard Hal tell him that many times over the years. How could he have forgotten such a simple truth?

"Your daddy is a smart man."

Adriana wiggled off the bed. "That's what he says about you, too."

Treat walked into the room with a grave look in his eyes. He scooped up Adriana. "Rex, it's Earl. He's back in the hospital."

Rex pushed past Treat and pulled out his cell. His big fingers fumbled with the screen as he called Jade.

"Rex?"

He heard the fear in her voice. "I'm here, baby. Where are you?"

"We're pulling into the driveway."

"I'm there." He blew past Treat and Hugh and bolted down the driveway.

Jade jumped from Max's car and ran into his open arms, sobbing. "You were right all along."

"Shh, baby. He's going to be okay." Rex wasn't a praying man, but on the way to the hospital with Jade pressed to his side and his heart in his throat, he prayed to anyone and anything willing to listen for Earl to be okay.

Chapter Ten

"ANGINA. SERIOUSLY, EARL?" Hal teased. "You couldn't do better than that? And you call me a sissy."

Rex knew his father was just trying to lighten the mood. Their entire family and their children, as well as Jade's mother and brother, were crammed into Earl's hospital room. They were keeping him overnight to monitor his heart rate, and Jade was a distraught mess. Rex wanted to get a few minutes alone with her, to reassure her that everything would be okay, but there were too many people.

Shannon was trying to keep the kids entertained with Max and Brianna near the doorway. They were playing with rubber gloves that Ben had made into balloons for them. Steven was eyeing Shannon with a look of lust in his eyes that made Rex want to smack him upside the head, and Treat and Hugh were huddled off to the side, talking with Savannah and Jack.

"Angina is still better than broken heart syndrome," Earl teased.

"I wish you did have broken heart syndrome, Earl. You scared the daylights out of me," Jane said.

Jade clung to Rex's chest and he cocooned her within his arms.

"What can I do, baby?" Rex asked. "I'm sorry about the wedding."

"It's okay. I should have listened to you in the first place. I don't even care anymore."

"Of course you care. You're just upset." Rex pulled her closer and kissed the top of her head.

"I'm scared," she whispered.

He felt his heart crack open. Her pain was his pain. Her sadness became his.

"He's going to be okay. You heard Ben."

"I shouldn't have put off planning the wedding for so long. I should have let you plan it."

"Don't be silly. You'll have your wedding, and it'll be every-thing you dreamed of." Rex's muscles corded tight, knowing that on top of her father being readmitted to the hospital, Jade's dream wedding had fallen apart.

"What you kids don't understand," Hal said, "is that none of that wedding crap matters."

"Dad," Rex warned. He didn't need a lecture or a joke. He wanted to give Jade the perfect wedding she deserved, and right now, he wanted to carry her out of this room and hold her until she felt better.

"Son, haven't I taught you anything over the years? Your love for Jade and her love for you is what matters. Love exists in our hearts. It can't be scheduled or created, and it sure as hell isn't stronger or better because you promise it will be in our backyard. Love just *is*, and that girl of yours knows how deep your love runs."

Hal set his large hand on Jade's shoulder. "Jade, your father is one stubborn bastard. He'll probably be around for another thirty years, but whether he walks you down the aisle or watches from a chair won't make your marriage to Rex mean any more than it would if you married him at the top of the Taj Mahal or in the middle of the desert. The sooner you kids learn that, the better."

Rex wiped tears from Jade's cheek. "I'm sorry, Jade."

"No. He's right." Jade covered Hal's hand with her own. "I know that. I'm just overwhelmed, and I'm sorry about the necklace, Hal. I know how special it was to you."

"Necklace?" Hal shifted his eyes to Rex in confusion.

"I...I lost the Dance of Two Lovers necklace."

Treat and Hugh moved between Jade and Hal, as if their presence might somehow protect her from whatever Hal's reaction might be.

"You didn't lose it. That necklace can't be lost," Hal said, surprising them all.

"Dad," Rex said, "we've looked everywhere." He tightened his grip on Jade.

Hal waved a hand. "Hear that, Earl? They've looked everywhere."

"Hey, one day they'll be old enough to be as smart as we are. Until then, humor them." Earl bought Jane's hand to his lips and pressed a kiss to it.

"It isn't lost, just like Hope wasn't sick." Hal ran a hand through his hair and shook his head.

She wasn't about to argue with Hal about something he loved so vehemently—that she *knew* was lost. Instead she simply apologized. "Well, I am sorry, and I hope I find it someday." Jade turned to Rex. "I love you."

Rex pressed his cheek to hers. "Baby, I love you more than words can express." He looked around the room. Treat and Hugh remained an unnecessary protective barrier between them and his father. He didn't need their protecting, but he took comfort knowing that if something were ever to happen to him, his brothers would step in and protect Jade from everyone and everything in his absence.

He watched Brianna rubbing noses with Christian while the little boy giggled. Layla and Adriana sat on chairs beside each other, flipping through books Max had magically pulled out of her purse. His sisters-in-law were amazing mothers, just as he knew Savannah and, someday, Jade would be. Jack's arm circled Savannah as they whispered something to each other. He wished Dane and Lacy were there, but no one had been able to reach them all day. Maybe his father was right and things didn't have to be perfect. They just had to *be*.

His mother's voice whispered through his mind again—*Dress*—and it spurred him into action.

"Hey, Treat. Can you take care of Jade for me for a few minutes? I have to go pick something up."

"'Course. Whatever you need." Treat stepped in beside Jade.

Rex lifted Jade's chin and pressed a kiss to her lips. "I forgot to call our cousins. They're probably wandering around the yard. I'll be back as fast as I can, okay?"

As Rex walked out the door, his father's hand landed on his shoulder. Rex stilled. His father gave him a quick nod of approval, as if he knew what Rex had in mind, which would be a miracle in and of itself, considering Rex wasn't even sure.

Chapter Eleven

"WHERE IS HE?" Jade checked the time again. "It's been almost two hours since Rex left."

"Did you give him your news yet?" Max shifted Dylan to her other hip.

"What news?" Treat asked.

"Nothing," they answered in unison.

"That's a whole lot of *something* in that *nothing*. Rex texted me a few minutes ago. He should be here any minute," Treat said. "Hugh, Jack, and I are going to grab something from the car. We'll be right back."

"Treat?" Max held a hand up in question.

He strode casually across the floor and reached for Dylan. "Want me to take him?"

"No. I'm just wondering what you guys need from the car."

"Oh." Treat looked at Jack, who looked at Hugh.

The right side of Hugh's lips quirked up in a crooked smile. "I have a surprise in the car for Jade and Rex, and I thought it would be a good time to give it to Jade." Hugh grabbed Treat's and Jack's arms and dragged them from the room.

"What the heck was that all about?" Max asked.

"Hey, he's your husband, not mine. Apparently, my future

husband thought now was the perfect time to disappear." Jade checked her phone again. She'd texted Rex twice but hadn't heard back.

"I learned a long time ago not to even to try to figure out a man. How much trouble can they get into in a hospital?" Savannah laughed and read a text message that had just vibrated through. "Jade, I have to return a call. I'll be back in a sec." Savannah left the room and came back and grabbed Hal. "Dad, I might need you."

"I think I'll take the kids to the bathroom now that there aren't so many people around." Brianna reached for Layla's hand. "Max? Shannon? Why don't we take them all at once and get it over with. Let's give Jade's family a little privacy."

With everyone gone except Steve and her parents, the room suddenly seemed *too* quiet. "Dad, do you want me to get you anything?" Jade asked.

"No, darlin'. I'm just fine. I'm sorry I messed up your wedding, honey."

"You didn't." Rex strode into the room and reached for Jade's hand. He had two garment bags draped over his shoulder. He tossed one across Earl's legs. "Put that on after we get out of here."

"What?" Earl grumbled, and snarled at the garment bag strewn across his legs.

"Where have you been?" Jade asked. "I've been texting you."

Rex guided her to the other side of the room and pulled the curtain closed separating them from her family.

"Rex?" she pushed.

"Take your clothes off, baby."

"Hey!" Earl growled from behind the curtain.

"I'm marrying her, Earl. Knock it off."

"Rex, what…?" Jade leaned on his shoulder as he pulled down her shorts and took them off, leaving her cowgirl boots on. Then he took her top off and carefully withdrew her beautiful wedding dress from the garment bag.

"Oh my God. Rex. What are you doing?"

"Marrying you. We don't need things to be perfect, Jade. We just need each other. I love you, and if you want to marry me, then put that hot little body of yours in that wedding dress. We don't have much time."

"Earl? You getting up out of that bed yet?" Rex hollered over his shoulder.

"For crying out loud," Earl grumbled again.

"I've already talked to Ben and gotten the okay. You're giving your daughter away. It'll take all of fifteen minutes, and then you can sit your ass down in that bed again. *Capisce?*"

"Get up, Earl. This is for your baby girl." Jane's excited voice cut straight to Jade's heart.

"Rexy?" Tears streamed down her cheeks as Rex helped her into her gown. "I secretly wanted to be married in my cowgirl boots. Riley will hate it. She went to so much trouble to design the perfect gown."

"Riley loves it. Trust me. Jade, if you still want a real wedding, I'll give you the biggest, best wedding you've ever dreamed of. But right here, right now, we're becoming man and wife."

She opened her mouth to tell him that she wouldn't want it any other way, but a lump had formed in her throat. He zipped up her dress and wiped her tears from her cheeks.

"There's only one way you could look more beautiful," he whispered.

She bit her lower lip and whispered, "Naked?"

"That's my dirty girl," he teased. He reached into his pocket and pulled out the Dance of Two Lovers necklace.

Jade sucked in a jagged breath as fresh tears tumbled down her cheeks.

"How? Where…?"

"It was stuck inside your dress. It must have gotten caught during your last fitting." He gathered her hair over one shoulder and hooked the necklace. "But I want you to know that even if we never found it, it wouldn't have changed a thing." He pressed his lips to hers.

Rex drew the curtain open, and Jade's father stood in his hospital gown with a dress coat over the top and hospital booties on his feet.

"I pinned the back closed," Jane said with a smile.

Jade laughed through her tears. "Daddy, you've never looked more handsome."

"Darlin'…" For the first time in her life, Jade saw tears running down her father's cheeks.

She wrapped her arms around him. "I love you."

"I love you, too, darlin'. Now, let's go get you married before this draft gets any colder."

"Give me ten seconds," Rex said, and touched Jade's arm as he disappeared into the hallway.

She heard the "Wedding March" playing, and her father smiled down at her.

"That's our cue, darlin'."

Jade stepped into the hallway, which was now lined with the flowers they'd ordered from the florist. All of Rex's cousins from Trusty and their significant others were there, lining the hall with wide smiles. Jade's bridesmaids stood up the hall to the left of Treat, who was officiating the ceremony. He'd been ordained years earlier in order to marry couples at his resorts. To his right were Rex's brothers, *including* Dane. Jade's eyes swept over the bridesmaids again, lingering on Lacy, who was glowing a little brighter than usual despite being sick.

Lacy splayed her left hand over her belly. She mouthed, *Baby! We eloped!* and pointed to the ring on her left finger.

Jade had no hope of stopping the river of tears that blurred the vision of her soon-to-be sister-in-law or the swell in her heart to know they'd be having babies around the same time.

Steve whispered something to Shannon that made her blush. Then he walked beside Dylan as he toddled down the aisle carrying a red velvet pillow that Jade knew had their rings attached with a safety pin. Shannon nudged Layla and Adriana, who scattered rose petals along the floor as they followed Steve and Dylan down the hall.

The aisle.

Our wedding aisle.

Our perfect wedding aisle.

"You can still back out," her father said quietly with a teasing smile.

"No chance in hell, Daddy."

Jade walked down the aisle on her father's arm, in her cowgirl boots and wedding gown. It didn't matter that there were a handful of nurses watching from behind a counter, or that her father wore a hospital gown and booties. All that mattered was that the handsome man at the end of the hall, the one who was looking at her like she was the most beautiful creature that walked the earth, with so much love in his eyes she felt her knees weaken, was about to become her husband.

And a father.

I'm going to be a mother. Jade faltered.

"You okay, darlin'?" her father asked.

"More than okay," she said honestly.

When they reached Rex, her father held her hands, and his eyes turned serious. "I couldn't be prouder than I am of the woman you've become. You're strong, smart, and stubborn, just like your old man. I adore you, baby girl, and it's with pleasure and pride that I give your hand in marriage to Rex. He's a good man." Earl shifted his eyes to Hal and added, "Like his old man."

Hal's eyes dampened.

Earl kissed Jade's cheeks, then lifted his chin to Rex. "Son."

How could one word pull more tears from the well she thought she'd run dry?

Rex took Jade's hand and he mouthed, *I love you.*

Jade mouthed, *I'm pregnant.*

Rex's mouth opened, his eyes widened, and then he swallowed hard. She nodded, and his eyes dropped to her belly. When he lifted them again, his eyes were as damp as hers. He gathered her in his arms and kissed her.

"Okay," Treat said with a laugh. "I guess we're doing things in reverse order."

"You're sure, babe?" Rex splayed his hand over her stomach. She nodded.

"I love you." He lifted her off her feet and kissed her again.

Treat cleared his throat.

"Sorry. Go ahead." Rex shifted nervously from foot to foot. He'd been smiling since Jade told him she was pregnant, and now, as his eyes shifted from her belly to her face to his father, then back again, she knew he could barely contain his excitement.

"Tha—"

Rex's arms shot up in the air, interrupting Treat. "We're

pregnant!" He beamed at Jade. "We're having a baby." Rex laughed as he scooped Jade into his arms again and kissed her, causing everyone to laugh and cheer.

"Rex!" Treat said. "Do you take Jade to be your bride?"

"Damn right I do." He never took his eyes off of Jade.

"Jade, do you take Rex to be your husband?" Treat couldn't have spoken faster if he'd tried.

"Forever and always." Jade barely got the words out before Rex sealed their vows with another soul-searing kiss, in a perfect wedding to the love of her life, right there in the hall of Weston Memorial Hospital, surrounded by those who loved them most.

—The End—

Chapter One

TREAT BRADEN DIDN'T usually charter planes. It wasn't his style to flash his wealth. But today he needed to be anywhere but his Nassau resort, and missing his commercial flight had just plain pissed him off. He owned upscale resorts all over the world, and he'd been featured on travel shows so many times that it turned his stomach to have to play those ridiculous media games. Lately, the pomp and circumstance surrounding him had begun to irk him in ways that it never had before meeting Max Armstrong. It had been too many long, lonely weeks since he'd seen her standing in the lobby of his Nassau resort, since his heart first thundered in a way that threw him completely off-kilter—and since they'd spent one incredible evening together. Treat wasn't a Neanderthal. He'd known he had no claim on her, even after their intimate evening. Hell, they hadn't even slept together. But that hadn't stopped his blood from boiling or kept him from acting like a jerk the next morning when he'd seen her with another man in front of the elevators, wearing the same clothes she'd had on when Treat had left her the night before.

He hadn't been able to stop thinking about Max since the moment he'd first met her, despite the uncomfortable encounter, but he'd been burned before, and he wasn't into repeating his mistakes. Getting away from resorts altogether and spending a weekend with his father at his ranch in Weston, Colorado, a small ranch town with dusty streets, too many cowboy hats, and a main drag that had been built to replicate the Wild West, was just what he needed.

His rental SUV moved at a snail's pace behind a line of traffic that was not at all typical for his hometown. It wasn't until he crawled around the next curve and saw balloons and banners above the road announcing the annual Indie Film Festival that he realized what weekend it was. He uttered a curse. He wasn't in the mood to deal with crowds.

His cell phone rang, and his sister's name flashed on the screen. Before he could say hello, Savannah said, "I can't believe you didn't tell me you were coming to town."

"Hi, sis. I miss you, too." The only girl among his five siblings, Savannah was a cutthroat entertainment attorney, but to Treat she'd always be his baby sister.

"When will you get into Weston?"

"I'm here now, sitting in traffic on Main Street." He hadn't moved an inch in five minutes.

"I'm at the festival with a client. Come see me."

All he really wanted to do was reach his father's two-hundred-acre ranch just outside of town, but Treat knew that if he didn't see Savannah right away, she'd be disappointed. Disappointing his siblings was something he strived not to do. Having lost their mother when Treat was only eleven and his youngest sibling, Hugh, had been hardly more than a baby, his siblings had already faced enough disappointment for one lifetime.

"You're with a client. Sure you can get away?" he asked.

"For you? Of course. Besides, I'm with Connor Dean. He can handle things for a little while. Come in the back gate. I'll wait there." Connor was an actor who was quickly climbing the ranks of fame. Savannah had been his attorney for two years, and whenever he had a public engagement, he brought her along. It wasn't a typical attorney-client relationship, but for all of Connor's bravado, he'd been slandered one too many times. Savannah kept track of what was and wasn't said at most events—by both Connor and the media.

"I'll be there as soon as traffic allows." After he ended the call with Savannah he called his father.

"Hey there, son."

Hal's slow, deep drawl tugged at Treat's heart. He'd missed him. Hal had always been a calming influence on Treat. After his mother passed away, his father had pulled him and his siblings through those tumultuous years. But Hal wasn't a coddler. He had instilled a strong work ethic and sense of loyalty into their heads, and that had enabled each of them to be successful in their endeavors.

"Dad, I'm here in town, but I'm going to stop at the festival first to see Savannah, if you don't mind."

"Yup. Savannah called. She misses you, and I'd venture a guess that you could use a little extended family time, too."

He could say that again. Anything to keep his mind off Max.

TREAT PULLED UP to the rear gate behind a mass of media surrounding a number of cars. He rolled down his window and was met with too many shouts to decipher. It was obvious no one was going anywhere anytime soon. He pulled into the parking lot outside the fence and decided he'd run in, say hello to Savannah, and tell her he'd catch up with her later at their father's ranch. The last thing he needed was to deal with this type of headache.

He heard his sister's voice and swiftly scanned the crowd. If anyone was giving her a hard time, he'd set them straight. Savannah was standing with her body out of a limousine's sunroof, shouting who knew what as the media hollered questions at Connor through the slightly open tinted limousine window.

Treat leaned against the entrance to the gate, crossed one foot over the other, and watched his little sister in action. Her long auburn hair looked like fire against her serious more-green-than-hazel eyes. She'd inherited their mother's spitfire personality and was the only one to have their mother's coloring, while he and his brothers took after their dark-haired father.

Savannah's gaze shifted in his direction, and her scowl morphed into an excited smile as she hoisted herself through the sunroof like she climbed mountains for a living.

Treat pushed away from the fence and headed toward his sister in full protective mode. She might be tough, but those media animals pushing their way forward could easily injure her. He plowed through the crowd. His six-foot-six frame naturally commanded more space, and the sea of paparazzi parted for him. He gently persuaded the few that remained in his path with a domineering stare—a stare he hadn't needed to rely upon since Savannah was a teenager, when he and his brothers had spent countless hours keeping horny boys away from their precious sister.

He reached up and caught Savannah as she jumped down from the roof of the limo. He spun her around and, as he lowered her to the ground, his eyes landed on a woman standing at the front of the line of cars waving her hands. Her dark hair was pulled back in a ponytail, her red-framed glasses perched on her perky nose. She looked fierce and beautiful, and Treat's breath caught in his throat. *Max.*

MAX ARMSTRONG STOOD beside her car waving her hands, hoping to create a long enough break in the excitement to gain control of the crowd. Chaz Crew, Max's boss and founder of the Indie Film Festival, had created so much buzz over the past few years that they were expecting more than forty thousand attendees. The festival grounds covered one hundred acres a few blocks from Main Street and boasted five new theaters, restaurants, gift shops, and a high-class hotel. Hotels in neighboring towns were booked a full year in advance of the festival. Whether there were twenty thousand or fifty thousand attendees, Max was ready. She'd been handling the festival sponsors and logistics for almost eight years, and nothing could throw her off her game. Not even the ruckus between the celeb's entourage and the media, which was creating a tornado of confusion.

Photographers surrounded Connor Dean's limousine and the two accompanying SUVs. Max should have known this might happen. Dean was a local actor turned millionaire whose reputation had exploded since they'd booked him ten months earlier. She'd been wrong to think the Hulk-like security guards could manage a little drama. Shouts and threats were tossed around like candy to children, and no one was making any headway. *What on earth is that woman doing with her body halfway out of the sunroof on that limo? And what is she shouting? Legal jargon?*

The heck with this. It was time for Plan B. She climbed onto the roof of her car, which she'd strategically parked in front of the first SUV. *This* was why she wore jeans and her usual festival T-shirt. Because crazy shit happened at festivals.

With a quick flip of a switch on the control panel on her belt, she turned on the intercom mounted above the gate. "Okay, the show is over." Her voice boomed from the loud-speakers. "Let's give Mr. Dean some space to continue driving through. He'll be signing autographs and answering questions after his appearance." She scanned the area, her gaze landing on a man towering above the crowd with a gorgeous woman in his arms. He spun the woman to the side and his face came into view.

Max froze.

Treat?

Her pulse soared, and the butterflies in her stomach she thought she'd annihilated weeks ago swarmed to life with a vengeance. She had worked with Treat's assistant, Scarlet, for months coordinating logistics for Chaz's double wedding, which had taken place at Treat's Nassau resort. The other groom in the wedding was Treat's cousin, Blake Carter. She'd dealt with Treat so many times over the phone that he'd become the object of her late-night fantasies. But even her fantasies hadn't prepared her for meeting the impossibly tall, darkly handsome god that was Treat Braden, with his seductive voice and the way every inch of him screamed of adrenaline-pumping, heart-fluttering masculinity. She'd thought herself unflappable, but Treat had proved her wrong.

Her entire body heated up just thinking about the magical evening they'd spent in each other's arms. She could still feel his eager arousal pressed against her as they danced, still taste his warm, sensuous lips, and she could still see him gazing at her as though she were the only woman on earth. He hadn't even pushed when, after hours of dancing and walking on the beach, kissing like they'd been lovers forever, she'd turned down his offer to return to his suite and extend their evening into morning. Seeing him now, she had a hard time reconciling that incredibly romantic, thoughtful man with the arrogant one who had blown her off the next morning. Sure, she'd been in the same clothes she'd worn the night before, and yes, she'd been out for the remainder of that evening with a man named Justin, but Treat's assumption about what they'd done pissed her off. And the look he'd given her was too reminiscent of the painful relationship she'd escaped years earlier to chase him down and explain. She had every right to do whatever she wanted to do with whomever she wanted, without judgment. Even if she hadn't done anything at all.

She shouldn't care what he thought.

But she did, and that hurt because that awful look he'd given her was in such stark contrast to the impeccable manners he'd otherwise exuded, holding doors, thinking of the needs of her and his other guests before himself, taking extra steps to ensure that every little detail of his cousin's wedding had been taken care of. The truth was, she'd fallen hard for Treat within a few hours of being with him. But Max knew she shouldn't let those feelings sway her resolve. She'd been mistreated, demeaned, and judged by a previous boyfriend, and she swore she'd never go down that road again—not even for too-sexy-for-his-own-good Treat Braden.

She stumbled backward. One of the security guards reached for her across the roof of the car, and she grabbed his arm, finding her footing.

"Max! You okay?"

The security guard's voice wrenched her back to the ensuing chaos. She tore her eyes from Treat and whoever the woman was that he was holding as if she meant everything in the world to him and tried to blink away the unexpected sting of hurt slicing through her.

"Clear a path or you'll be removed from the premises for the rest of the festival." Even she could hear the difference in her voice, the weakness. Her gaze darted back to Treat, who was staring at her with an incredulous expression. Suddenly painfully aware of her jeans and T-shirt, the ponytail in her hair—and how she must look like a crazy woman standing on top of the car—she clambered down to the ground as the crowd surprisingly obeyed her orders and began to dissipate. Threats of eviction usually worked.

She turned off the intercom and fumbled for her keys. Treat was heading her way, but she didn't want to speak to him, couldn't speak to him, after the way he'd looked at her.

"Max," he called.

His rich, deep voice was enough to make her body ache. She cursed under her breath as she started the car and navigated around the crowd. She glanced in her rearview mirror. Treat stood alone in his dark suit, staring after her, while his beautiful companion looked on with a confused expression on her face.

Max's hands trembled as she grasped the steering wheel tighter and drove away.

To continue reading, please buy LOVERS AT HEART, REIMAGINED

SHOP.MELISSAFOSTER.COM

Sign up for Melissa's newsletter to stay up to date on new releases.

www.MelissaFoster.com/Newsletter

CONNECT WITH MELISSA

FACEBOOK:

Facebook.com/MelissaFosterAuthor

WEBSITE:

www.MelissaFoster.com

READER GROUP:

Facebook.com/groups/MelissaFosterFans

SHOP MELISSA'S STORE:

SHOP.MELISSAFOSTER.COM

More Books By Melissa

<u>LOVE IN BLOOM BIG-FAMILY ROMANCE COLLECTION</u>

SNOW SISTERS
Sisters in Love
Sisters in Bloom
Sisters in White

THE BRADENS at Weston
Lovers at Heart, Reimagined
Destined for Love
Friendship on Fire
Sea of Love
Bursting with Love
Hearts at Play

THE BRADENS at Trusty
Taken by Love
Fated for Love
Romancing My Love
Flirting with Love
Dreaming of Love
Crashing into Love

THE BRADENS at Peaceful Harbor
Healed by Love
Surrender My Love
River of Love
Crushing on Love
Whisper of Love
Thrill of Love

THE BRADENS & MONTGOMERYS at Pleasant Hill – Oak Falls
Embracing Her Heart
Anything for Love

Trails of Love
Wild Crazy Hearts
Making You Mine
Searching for Love
Hot for Love
Sweet Sexy Heart
Then Came Love
Rocked by Love
Falling for Mr. Bad

THE BRADENS at Ridgeport
Playing Mr. Perfect
Sincerely, Mr. Braden

THE BRADEN NOVELLAS
Promise My Love
Our New Love
Daring Her Love
Story of Love
Love at Last
A Very Braden Christmas

THE REMINGTONS
Game of Love
Stroke of Love
Flames of Love
Slope of Love
Read, Write, Love
Touched by Love

THE RYDERS
Seized by Love
Claimed by Love
Chased by Love
Rescued by Love
Swept Into Love

SEASIDE SUMMERS

Seaside Dreams
Seaside Hearts
Seaside Sunsets
Seaside Secrets
Seaside Nights
Seaside Embrace
Seaside Lovers
Seaside Whispers
Seaside Serenade

BAYSIDE SUMMERS

Bayside Desires
Bayside Passions
Bayside Heat
Bayside Escape
Bayside Romance
Bayside Fantasies

THE STEELES AT SILVER ISLAND

Tempted by Love
My True Love
Caught by Love
Always Her Love
Wild Island Love
Enticing Her Love

THE SILVERS AT SILVER ISLAND

Flirting with Trouble
The Trouble with Flings

THE WHISKEYS: DARK KNIGHTS AT PEACEFUL HARBOR

Tru Blue
Truly, Madly, Whiskey
Driving Whiskey Wild
Wicked Whiskey Love
Mad About Moon

Taming My Whiskey
The Gritty Truth
In for a Penny
Running on Diesel

THE WHISKEYS: DARK KNIGHTS AT REDEMPTION RANCH
The Trouble with Whiskey
Freeing Sully (Prequel to For the Love of Whiskey)
For the Love of Whiskey
A Taste of Whiskey
Love, Lies, and Whiskey
My Whiskey Redemption

THE WICKEDS: DARK KNIGHTS AT BAYSIDE
A Little Bit Wicked
The Wicked Aftermath
Crazy, Wicked Love
The Wicked Truth
His Wicked Ways
Talk Wicked to Me
Irresistibly Wicked

WILD BOYS AFTER DARK
Logan
Heath
Jackson
Cooper

BAD BOYS AFTER DARK
Mick
Dylan
Carson
Brett

SUGAR LAKE
The Real Thing
Only for You

Love Like Ours
Finding My Girl (Graphic Companion Booklet)

HARMONY POINTE
Call Her Mine
This is Love
She Loves Me

SILVER HARBOR
Maybe We Will
Maybe We Should
Maybe We Won't

STANDALONE ROMANTIC COMEDIES
Hot Mess Summer
The Mr. Right Checklist

HARBORSIDE NIGHTS SERIES
Includes characters from the Love in Bloom series
Catching Cassidy
Discovering Delilah (F/F)
Tempting Tristan (M/M)

More Books by Melissa
Chasing Amanda (mystery/suspense)
Come Back to Me (mystery/suspense)
Have No Shame (historical fiction/romance)
Love, Lies & Mystery (3-book bundle)
Megan's Way (literary fiction)
Traces of Kara (psychological thriller)
Where Petals Fall (suspense)

Acknowledgments

It was such a joy to be back in Rex and Jade's world and to catch up with our lovable Bradens! I'd like to thank my readers for pushing me to tell Rex and Jade's wedding story sooner rather than later, and a big thank-you to Lynn Mullan and Kristen Weber for our brainstorming sessions.

We have many more Bradens to look forward to with the Peaceful Harbor and Pleasant Hills Braden love stories on the horizon. To keep up to date on my upcoming releases, please sign up for my newsletter www.MelissaFoster.com/Newsletter and check out the Reader Goodies page for a downloadable family tree, publication schedule, Love in Bloom merchandise, and more. You can also follow me on Facebook to see pictures of our hunky heroes and sexy heroines and to hear about my latest projects. Facebook.com/MelissaFosterAuthor

I am indebted to my amazing team of editors and proof-readers, whose meticulous efforts help bring you the cleanest books possible. Thank you: Kristen Weber, Penina Lopez, Jenna Bagnini, Juliette Hill, Marlene Engel, and Lynn Mullan. Thank you, Natasha Brown, for the gorgeous cover.

And, of course, thank you to my family for being my biggest inspiration of all.

Meet Melissa

www.MelissaFoster.com

Melissa Foster is the *New York Times*, *Wall Street Journal*, and *USA Today* bestselling and award-winning author of more than 100 novels. Her books have been recommended by *USA Today*'s book blog, *Hagerstown* magazine, *The Patriot*, and several other print venues.

Melissa enjoys discussing her books with book clubs and reader groups and welcomes an invitation to your event. Melissa's books are available through most online retailers in paperback, digital, and audio formats.

Melissa also writes sweet romance under the pen name Addison Cole.

9 781941 480144